FAMILY WAY

A LUNGHI FAMILY NOVEL

FAMILY WAY

MICHAEL Z. LEWIN

FIVE STAR
A part of Gale, Cengage Learning

GALE
CENGAGE Learning·

Detroit • New York • San Francisco • New Haven, Conn • Waterville, Maine • London

LIBRARY OF CONGRESS CATALOGING-IN-PUBLICATION DATA

Lewin, Michael Z.
    Family way : a Lunghi family novel / Michael Z. Lewin. — 1st ed.
        p. cm.
    ISBN-13: 978-1-4328-2542-3 (hardcover)
    ISBN-10: 1-4328-2542-9 (hardcover)
    1. Private investigators—England—Fiction. 2. Murder—Investigation—Fiction. 3. Bath (England)—Fiction. I. Title.
PS3562.E929F44 2011
813'.54—dc23   2011033160

First Edition. First Printing: December 2011.
Published in 2011 in conjunction with Tekno Books and Ed Gorman.

Printed in the United States of America
1 2 3 4 5 6 7 15 14 13 12 11

FAMILY WAY

1

"Where are you off to?" Angelo Lunghi asked his daughter, Marie, as they headed down the stairs from the family's flat.

"I'm meeting Cassie."

"Seeing the sights?"

"I *don't* think so, Pa."

Angelo was surprised. It was not a normal day on Walcot Street and the sights would be special ones. One Sunday every year the people of "The Republic of Walcot" declared independence from the city of Bath and the nation of Great Britain. With a motto of "Walcot Waives the Rules," the street was closed to traffic and there was a huge party. The world and its friends bought entry "passports" and poured in to listen to music, shop at the stalls, dance with parading revellers, eat exotic foods, and drink, drink, drink.

"It's so *not* me," Marie told her father.

The Lunghis' home and business were in the centre of these yearly parties so there was nothing new about Nation Day in principle, but, even so, something about Marie's insouciance struck Angelo as odd. Was she up to something?

Silly question. Teenagers were *always* up to something.

"Meeting Cassie, not your boyfriend?"

"*What* boyfriend, Pa?"

"Worth a try," Angelo said. Although . . . hadn't there been talk of some boy recently? Or was that just David trying to wind up his older sister?

"You are *so* lame," Marie said, but she was smiling. "And where are *you* going on Nation Day *without* Mum?"

"I'm off to see a new client."

"On a Sunday?"

"The client calls and wants a detective today." He spread his hands. It was out of his control.

"I'm *never* going to work." Marie tossed her hair and opened the front door.

The wave of music from outside was all but a physical one. The Nation's main stage was directly opposite the Lunghis' home and work. The open door revealed a mass of watching and dancing people that was almost solid.

Marie slid out and headed left, toward the city centre. Angelo followed, closing the door securely behind him. That's *all* the rest of the family upstairs would need—strangers spreading out to fill available spaces, parking themselves on the stairs for a rest, heedless of whose stairs they were. Waiving the rules of normal behaviour.

Marie was not far ahead of him, but Angelo struggled to catch up because he could only go as fast as the current of people he was a part of. He managed to get close because she stopped for a moment to watch a giraffe and a giant goose bop together to the band. So she was not *entirely* immune to the Nation Day sights . . .

And there was something to be said for stilt-walking. You might suffocate as the sun beat down on a silly costume, but at least you could see over the heads of the seething citizenry and decide which was the best route to get you to where you were going.

Angelo was about to tap Marie on the arm when something hit him on the side of his forehead. He jerked back and touched his head where it had been hit. He found something sticky and wet. Looking at his fingers showed it was red. Not blood, though. It was jam. Someone was throwing *jam?*

It had come from above, so he looked up. The shops along this part of the street projected out from the upper storeys by perhaps a yard. Angelo saw several sets of feet dangling over the edge. One young man waved an apology with one hand while showing a doughnut with the other. Some of the filling had leaked out.

That's all I need, Angelo thought. To arrive at Mrs. Wigmore's with jam on my face. He'd have to go back and wash.

But before he could move into the current of people that was moving toward home, a tall young woman with rings dangling from her nose and hair dyed a rainbow of colours pulled him close and licked his forehead. It was over before he took in what was happening. She stepped away again and dried his head with a tissue. "All better now," she said.

"Excuse *me*," Marie said, now beside her father. "Just what was *that* about?"

Angelo turned back to ask the stranger to explain, but the rainbow woman was gone. "I . . . It . . ."

Marie laughed. "Give me a fiver and I won't tell Mum."

"It . . . I . . ."

"Give me a tenner and I *will* tell Mum."

A Nation Day adventure. Angelo laughed too.

"Bye, Pa."

"Wait, Marie."

"What?"

"When will you be home?"

"How do I know?"

"It *is* a school night."

"*Pa!* It's two-thirty in the afternoon!!"

And, yes, perhaps a little early to be fretting. But kids, especially Marie, take advantage. "You have your phone?"

"Of *course*. Duh."

"And you'll be back for supper?"

Marie tossed her hair. "Will David be back for supper?"

"I expect so."

"But you don't *know?*"

"Not for sure. Why?"

"So it's just *me,* the *daughter,* the *girl,* who gets the third-degree and the shackles?"

"It's not like that," Angelo said.

"Seems like it to me," Marie said.

"Well, David certainly doesn't prance off to God knows where flaunting his belly-button ring."

"*Prance?* You want me to *prance?*" Marie hitched her bag over one shoulder and *pranced* toward town, leaving her father to watch as several young men's eyes followed her departure.

He sighed, knowing he'd handled it badly. Or at least that he hadn't extracted the information or promises that he'd wanted. It was the curse of the father of a teenage girl. Her mother would say, "Trust her," but Marie had got herself into scrapes in the past. And Gina didn't really *know* what it was like to be a sex-crazed young man. Angelo, alas, did.

But there was a client to visit. He set out again, walking both because it was a lovely day and because it would be all but impossible to get a car out with Walcot Street closed. He touched his forehead where the jam had hit. It felt clean. He could check his reflection in a window or a mirror somewhere along the way. But the rainbow woman *had* pronounced him all better now. He smiled.

People were still pouring into the street as he passed the "passport" checkpoint. Young, old, families. As well as creatures, clowns and cowboys. Actors from the Natural Theatre Company had dressed as traffic wardens and were walking around with chairs trying to *get* people to "park" themselves—on the chairs—for a minute or two, in an inversion of the real wardens' job.

The Naturals' little joke. If someone could think of it, on Nation Day someone did it. As Angelo passed the YMCA he stepped aside for a cluster of butterflies who were helping each other on with their wings.

Marie was nowhere in sight.

Mama, Angelo's mother, sat at her daughter-in-law's kitchen table, nursing a cup of tea. She was listening to the music pouring from the Nation Day main stage speakers through the flat's closed windows and solid walls. "Noise," Mama said. "It's all endless *noise.*"

"I like some of it," Gina said. She pushed a plate closer to her mother-in-law. "Another biscuit?"

"No no."

"What about the community choir? I thought you liked them." Gina took a chocolate digestive for herself. Nation Day *was* kind of a holiday. A time to waive the rules.

Mama sighed as she cast her mind back to the a cappella choir that began the music on the main stage. "They were sweet enough, I suppose." She too took a chocolate digestive.

"Sweet? You were dancing to them when you came in."

Mama shrugged and dunked. "But to listen to their idea of 'world music' you'd never know that we have music in *Italy*. Such beautiful songs, we have. But no. For this choir the 'world' is only elsewhere." She looked at her watch. "How much *longer*, Gina?"

"They have bands playing until about seven, I think."

"*Hours* yet." Mama was despairing. "And for this, for *this*—" She threw her arms toward the source of the samba music currently filling the room. "For *this* we miss our dinner?" On normal Sundays the extended Lunghi family gathered for a midday meal.

"Nation Day is only once a year," Gina said. "And the

11

children love it."

Mama considered. "Rosetta does seem enthusiastic," she said, thinking of her own children, rather than Gina's two. "That she should volunteer for their committee, to organize it for them."

Gina might have pointed out that as a new member of a large committee Rosetta was not likely to have been one of the event's movers or shakers. Instead, she sipped from her teacup and nibbled her biscuit.

Mama said, "Is there a man?"

"Excuse me?"

"For Rosetta to show such joining. Is that why my girl works so hard to make sure we have noise outside our house?"

"She hasn't mentioned anyone."

"I *hope* there's a man."

The love life of her two unmarried children was a subject Mama returned to daily. But since Gina had no information to contribute, she said, "What's *your* man up to, Mama?"

"Upstairs he gets ready to go to his gym to stay strong, but I will send him to the supermarket first."

"He's really taken to the gym," Gina said.

"It helps his brain as well as his body, you know."

Mama was about to continue but Gina held up a hand. "We'll give him work to do just as soon as we have something that's appropriate. Things are slow at the moment, but I've talked it through with Angelo and he's agreed."

"You're a good girl, Gina."

"Angelo's even gone out today, to talk to a prospective client."

Mama topped her teacup from the pot. "And my Rosetta is a good girl too. At least she *tries*. What do you think, Gina? If this committee works for Rosetta, then maybe Salvatore could join? They must have eligible women on this committee. And a woman who can *organize?* What better thing could there be for a painter than to have a wife who can run a household?" Salvatore, Mama's other unmarried child, her eldest, was a painter and only worked as a detective when it suited him.

But Gina didn't answer the rhetorical question. Instead, she shared a moment with Mama as they both suffered anew for Salvatore. So long a fickle heartbreaker, just after Christmas Salvatore had lost the only woman they'd ever known him truly to care about. This woman, this Heather, had just vanished before the turn of the new year, taking her baby with her. She'd upped and left, without warning, explanation or information about where she was going. Could that *really* have been what had happened?

The family had met Heather several times, and celebrated the birth of her daughter. Not Salvatore's genetically, but a baby he doted on, a baby maybe named partly after him. Heather was a bit of a hippie, but how could she just take little Salvia away without telling Salvatore *anything* about where they were going? Or was it just that Salvatore didn't want to talk about what he'd been told, didn't want to agonize in front of the rest of the family? But it was now five months since he'd announced Heather's departure with Salvia. Could he keep it all inside himself forever?

The Odd Down Sambsters launched into a new song, swamping the sound of the two women's sighs.

David Lunghi, too, heard the Odd Down Sambsters and swayed to their rhythm. However, as he walked along Walcot Street, Angelo and Gina's younger child was not headed for his home across from the mock-Brazilians. Instead, he was using the observational skills he had learned and honed as he grew up in a family of private detectives. Surveying the stalls and displays and street acts and stages that lined both sides of the Republic of Walcot's quarter-mile, David was listing the *most* entertaining and unusual of the Nation Day offerings.

However, this compilation of the day's top delights was not for his own pleasure. It was for a higher purpose. Sometime after three he was due to meet Lara Tonkin. David had a *date*.

Lara, Lara, Lara . . . Newly arrived from Cornwall, not only was Lara Tonkin *gorgeous,* she was an unexpected star—possibly even competitor—in David's computer class at school. David had no idea why this vision of loveliness had transferred to Bath with only six weeks of term remaining, but he wasn't complaining.

Nor did he complain when Miss Hamlish asked him to leave what he was doing to show the newcomer around the school's equipment. From the start it was as if he and Lara had known each other for years.

That was Wednesday. A day he would never forget. Through the remainder of the week he'd introduced her to more and more of the school's idiosyncrasies. So what could be more natural than that he should offer to show the beautiful little Cornish newcomer around one of the highlights of the year in her new city? "Sounds great," she said with a big smile on Friday when he'd finally found the nerve to invite her. "I won't be able to get there till sometime after three, but just tell me where to find you."

David elected to meet in front of a Norwegian furniture store at the southernmost end of the street. That way they could walk the full length of the event together. And then back again. David sighed whenever he thought about it.

When Lara said yes, he'd given her a passport that he'd purchased ahead in case she accepted. "Here's one I prepared earlier," he said. "Cool," she said as she looked over the map and list of events inside. And then she'd kissed him on the cheek, right there, in the hall, in front of at least nine people and a teacher. David relived the precious moment time and again.

David's grandfather, the Old Man, was not making a list but he was studying one. The shopping Mama had given him to do was not your ordinary shopping. The nearby supermarket was fine, good in fact, for most things. But less common products required a visit to the speciality shops—fresh bread from Parkhurst's; pork, leek and ginger sausages from The Sausage Shop; and today she wanted biscuits from Ben's Cookies. The task was made harder because it was a Sunday. Shopping in central Bath wasn't nearly as limited on a Sunday as it used to be but some places were still shut. It all had to be weighed up carefully and the optimum route chosen.

On most days he'd also be considering whether to shop before he went to the gym, or after. But places that were open on Sunday often weren't open as late as on other days, so shopping before the gym was the only option today. And the walk around the centre would serve to warm his muscles for the gym and shopping beforehand also meant he could go straight home for his shower.

Humming along with the music from the street he packed extra towels in his gym bag. These he could use to wrap some of his purchases separately and keep them warmer or cooler while they were stored in his locker.

Yes, that would make the best of this assignment he'd been given, this job. Making Mama happy, but also serving his own needs.

Angelo too had considered his route through central Bath carefully, but his concern had been to find somewhere along the way where he could check his forehead in the mirror. This he accomplished at British Home Stores, and there he saw clearly that no visible residue remained from the jam that had been dropped on him. He also saw a bed that rather appealed to him. It was large and the French-walnut frame was shaped to make the whole thing look like a basket, and rather inviting. It was totally inappropriate for Gina's and his bedroom but it was rare for furniture of any kind to appeal to Angelo so he paused beside it. What he *actually* wanted was to be in it, in the dark, asleep. He doubted, however, whether the store would be willing to allow him such a test-drive. And besides, he was on his way to Widcombe.

Leaving the store, Angelo used a corridor through the Southgate Shopping Centre to get to the railway station and the footbridge behind it that connected the banks of the Avon. After negotiating the ring road and climbing a bit of Widcombe Hill, he arrived at the address he'd been given by Mrs. Veronica Wigmore.

It was a modest terrace house facing the city. Probably it had good views from the upstairs rooms. From ground level, however, the view was only of the terrace facing. Angelo rang the bell.

He didn't have to wait for long. A short, stocky woman in her late forties and with short grey curly hair opened the door. "Mrs. Wigmore?"

"Thank you so much for coming out, Mr. Lunghi," she said.

"Not at all." Angelo could see the relief in the woman's face. Relief from what was yet to be revealed but being able to solve problems for people was one of the good things about being a detective. "Your message said you need some help."

"You and your family were *so* good at proving our Keith's wife was conning him, I thought if anybody could explain it, you could."

Keith Wigmore, her son, had been involved in a messy divorce from a wife called Kitten. Angelo and Gina had reviewed the case notes before he came out.

"The police won't help," Mrs. Wigmore said. "Oh, they showed up fast enough when they thought they might catch Des red-handed, but as soon as they found out he's *already* in jail, they couldn't care less."

"Hang on, hang on. Des?"

"Des is my husband."

"And he's in jail?"

"In Langnorton. North of the M4. Do you know it?"

"*Of* it, yes." Langnorton was a minimum-security prison and remand centre.

"It's Des's fourth time. Sometimes when I visit he calls it his holiday home, but I think he just says that to keep my spirits up. I was meant to be going up there today but the guards are in some management dispute so visiting was cancelled. And anyway I felt it was more important to talk with you."

So this wasn't going to be about wrongful imprisonment. "Why did the police come looking for him?"

"Because of the break-in at Crazy Coffee last Friday." Mrs. Wigmore shook her grey curls. "I'm getting this all confused. And I'm *so* sorry to have called you on a Sunday morning. And *this* Sunday especially."

"This Sunday?"

"Your family's home and business is on Walcot Street, isn't it? We used to live in the neighbourhood ourselves so I know what a big local event Nation Day is."

"We don't take part in Nation Day as a business, Mrs. Wigmore. And if we weren't happy to send someone out today, we wouldn't have checked our messages."

Happy was perhaps not the most accurate word, but clients are clients and work is work, especially when things are a bit quiet. If there was anything that the Old Man had taught his three children about the detective business it was that the clients' needs come first. As long as they can pay.

"You're very gracious about coming out," Mrs. Wigmore said, "and here I am being very rude."

"You are?"

"By keeping you out here on the step. Please come in." She moved back. "Would you care for a cup of coffee? Or tea?"

Marie was outside too but she had no intention of leaving her bench for such a thing as a cup of coffee or tea. The bench—on the high pavement across from the top of Milsom Street—faced south and she was enjoying the warmth of the June sunshine. She was also enjoying being cool as her best friend Cassie asked a series of questions.

"So he *hasn't* said he loves you yet?"

"He doesn't have to say it," Marie said. "It's obvious. Like *so* many men, he worships at my feet."

Cassie was waiting with Marie as Marie waited for Jason. Like her younger brother, Marie had a *date.*

"You are *so* lucky," Cassie said.

"Do you think it's luck," Marie asked, "or simply my fate?" She tossed her hair and uncrossed her legs before recrossing them the other way. In fact, she did feel lucky that someone like Jason wanted to go out with her, although she was not all that certain about his feelings. However, she had an image to maintain with Cassie, who was almost exactly Marie's age but didn't yet look it.

So it was no wonder that it was Marie who had attracted an older man. Jason was only a few weeks short of eighteen while Cassie had to settle for more juvenile attentions. Her Neil was not only their own age, but he was so immature and uncool that he actually wanted to spend the day on Walcot Street rather than hang in the city. When Jason did finally show up Cassie would be going to Nation Day and finding Neil just to have

18

something to do. Poor Cassie. Where did it all go wrong for her?

"It's *how* the burglar broke in, you see, Mr. Lunghi," Mrs. Wigmore said. "Would you like some Battenberg if you're not going to have any biscuits? I've got some Battenberg."

"No, thank you." Angelo tapped a pen on his notebook. "You said the break-in was at Crazy Coffee. We're talking about the café on Saracen Street, just around the corner from Walcot, yes?"

"That's the one."

"So how *did* the burglar break in?"

"Through the roof." Mrs. Wigmore sat back and looked up. Angelo's eyes followed hers, but there was nothing but a bare ceiling above them. "He drilled four holes and then cut out a square by sawing between them. Crazy Coffee has a flat roof, you see." She nodded to emphasize the significance. "At least let me top your tea."

Angelo's silence as he visualized the hole in Crazy Coffee's roof was taken as thirst by his prospective new client. She refilled his teacup from her cosy-covered pot. "Thank you," he said. "He *sawed* out a square?"

"That's why the police thought of Des. Because that's Des's MO. One time a judge even said it seemed to her that Des would pass up an open door in order to go in through a roof."

Angelo made notes and tried to absorb what he'd been told.

"Mind you," Mrs. Wigmore said, "I blame myself."

"I don't blame you," Laurence East said to Rosetta as they joined the crowds in Walcot Street.

"I hope not," Rosetta said.

"I wouldn't want to face a gang of girls alone either. I think gangs of girls can be scarier than gangs of boys."

Rosetta wasn't sure about that, but she was certainly pleased to be answering the security call with Laurence. He was so big and strong, like a rugby player—quite unlike the lithe, wiry men who'd caught her eye in the past. "I just didn't want to go by myself," she said.

They crossed to the eastern side of the street as they neared Cobham Court. "If you're dealing with a bloke," Laurence said, "you can give him a shove or two if you have to, and you both know where you stand. But it's so dodgy these days to touch a woman for any reason, even if it's in a public place."

Rosetta wasn't quite sure what to make of that. Maybe, with his size, Laurence was often challenged by other men. But women? She hardly knew anything about him because this was the first time they had been alone during the whole Nation Day planning process. If walking together through thousands of people really constituted being "alone."

When they rounded the corner that Walcot Street made with Cobham Court, Rosetta immediately recognized the problem they'd been called out to deal with. Half a dozen teenage girls, dressed almost completely in black, were rocking a section of the metal barrier that stretched across the street. Even above the noise of a disco stage not far away on Walcot Street, Rosetta could hear the girls screeching to cheer each other on.

The barrier had been supplied by the Nation Day Committee to help residents of the quiet cul-de-sac prevent their front steps and gardens being drenched in party urine and vomit as the day went on. But the only residents defending the barrier were two women. They both looked distressed.

Although one was old and small, she glared ferociously at the teenagers even as she backed away from them. The other woman held a walkie-talkie and must have been the person who radioed Security HQ for help. The walkie-talkie woman was tall, of indeterminate age and quite beautiful. Instinctively Rosetta glanced at Laurence to see if he was reacting to her but Laurence's concentration was on the gang of girls.

So it was Rosetta who went to speak with the walkie-talkie woman. "At last," the woman said.

"What's the problem?" Rosetta asked. Which was silly. She could see what the problem was. "I mean, how did it start?"

"One of the girls claims she has a friend down the street and wants to go there and change her top. Change her top? Change to what? From black to black? Look at them."

Rosetta saw what the walkie-talkie woman meant. All the girls wore black tops and most of them black jeans as well, as if it was a uniform or gang colours.

The walkie-talkie woman said, "Gloria told the girl, 'You'll have to come up with a better story than that to get through *this* gate.' "

"That's Gloria?" Rosetta indicated the small, angry old woman who was now waving her fist at the girls as Laurence tried to secure the top of the barrier.

"She's a pint in a sherry glass, Gloria," the beautiful walkie-talkie woman said. "I wish I had half her energy. But instead of going away, the girl rallied her friends and they started on the barrier. So I radioed for help. Thanks for coming."

"Of course."

"But is it just you and the big man? Because I don't know if you'll be enough. Your friend already seems to be in a bit of trouble."

The girls were circling Laurence now, and taunting him. They were cawing at him like a murder of crows.

Rosetta thought that she really ought to go help him. But the truth was she was frightened. So she stood where she was, uncertain what to do next. What would her father do in a situation like this?

2

It was half past three when the Old Man emerged from the Lunghis' house and faced the partying throngs. He paused to look at the men with saxophones and trumpets and funny hats on the main stage across the street. Their "music" sounded screechy to him, but the roadway was filled with dancers and bobbers and listeners who seemed to be enjoying themselves. And higher up too, people out on balconies and sitting in windows, all watching, listening, looking happy.

Fun and eating and listening to the music were all well and good but routines were still routines and jobs were still jobs. Even a stilt man pretending to be a knight on his charger should know that. You don't get anywhere in this life without plans you stick to. Or by letting people knock you from your course with a cardboard jousting sword, even if he does say, "Sorry." The Old Man turned left, toward the city centre. But to make any progress he had to find a stream of people flowing in the direction he wanted.

Slowly, the stream led him past the stage and several small shops and toward the passport control at the end of the street. But before he got there, he noticed David. The boy was leaning against a furniture shop window with his head down. Slumped, he looked. Was something wrong?

"David," the Old Man called, but there was no reaction. Well, how could there be, with all the noise? For his grandson he would be deflected. For his grandson he would leave the flow and head for the shore. So he did. And he was almost standing in front of David before the boy even saw him. "What is this? You ran out of breath and couldn't make it home?"

But David jumped up and away from the window, so maybe not out of breath after all. "Hi Grandpa."

"Hi, is it? I thought you were worn out and tired. Why else would you prop up that window?"

"I'm waiting for a friend. We're supposed to meet here." The boy gestured to the table in front of the shop from which they were selling some kind of food. What would they sell from a furniture shop? Boiled chairs? Huh!

But then the Old Man remembered something about a friend and David in the talk around the house, though he didn't remember quite what. And now David was standing, he seemed excited. That was good. A boy should have a friend.

The Old Man had had a friend, back in the Piedmontese village he and Mama had been born in. Long dead now, but he was a wonderful boyhood friend to explore the countryside with and throw stones. His name was Salvatore and the Old Man had named his first-born son after him.

"Grandpa?" David said.

"A friend is good for you to have," the Old Man said.

"Are you going to the gym?"

The Old Man held up his gym bag. "A reasonable deduction. But first I shop, for your grandmother. Perhaps I'll walk farther doing that than on the treadmill."

"Everybody says how much fitter you are these days," David said.

"What is the point for me to have more breath if your grandmother never lets me use it to talk back?"

David smiled. Then the Old Man saw the boy flick his eyes around. He turned to see what the boy was looking at, but it was just people. Ah, but he was expecting his friend. "Friends are good," he said. "I miss him."

"Who?"

"Salvatore."

"Uncle Sal? Is he here?"

"No, of course not." The Old Man was about to explain that Salvatore was long dead when he realized that David meant his *uncle*. Which is what he said. The older brother of his father, Angelo. So instead the Old Man said, "And if your father never lets me use my new breath by giving me a case to work on, what's the point? I could watch television all day instead."

"Well, I hope you keep going to the gym," David said. "Because you look better too. Even *I* can see that."

"You really think?" The Old Man made a mock display of a bicep.

"Impressive, Grandpa."

"You too could be a specimen. Come to the gym with me sometime. I can introduce you, show you the machines."

"Maybe I will in a few weeks, once school's out," David said. "If I have time."

The Old Man was about to say that you make your own time in this life, but he caught something in his grandson's expression. Was this a secret smile? Did David already have plans for his time in the summer? Well why not? "Now I am off, to do shopping for your grandmother and go to the YMCA." He put his hand out to pat his grandson on the head but David ducked away.

"I'm not a child anymore," David said.

The last thing the girl children at the Cobham Court barrier had in mind was ducking away. Whatever restriction of drunken movement had been achieved by the metal barrier, neither the committee nor the local residents had anticipated that the line of defence would be most seriously attacked by a flock of aggressive *girls*. Laurence's big hands just about kept it upright but at the same time he seemed to shrink away as the brashest of the girls pushed herself toward him and screamed, "What right do you have to keep me from going down a public street? What *right?*"

Rosetta could see that the girl's screamed questions were not likely to lead to a reasoned debate. Indeed, the girl moved in even closer, challenging the shrinking big man to stop her from going wherever the hell she wanted. The girl's *"What are you going to do about it? Eh? Eh?"* was heard even above the nearby sound stage.

But it was Rosetta, not Laurence, who *did* something. From her handbag she pulled out her mobile. She flicked it open and stepped forward and began to take pictures with it. From different positions and facing different girls she took picture after picture.

The brash screamer didn't notice at first, but others in the group did. One, smaller than the rest, moved away but Rosetta made sure to point the phone the girl's way and snap.

In moments the focus of the crowding crows was no longer on Laurence. It was on Rosetta.

"Did you just take my *picture?*" one asked.

"Yes," Rosetta said.

"Why?" The voice got louder.

"Because I wanted to." Snap, another picture.

"I'm not with them," the smaller one said, pushing her way between two others. "I was just here."

"Good," Rosetta said. Snap.

"So why did you take *my* picture?"

"Because you are intimidating the women who were minding the barrier."

"*I* wasn't doing that."

"You were with the group that was." Rosetta snapped the girl again. The not-with-them girl frowned, but couldn't think of anything to do but move away. That gave Rosetta a better view of the other girls. Snap. Snap.

By now the brash girl had pushed to the front. Rosetta lifted the phone, aimed at the girl's nose, and pushed the button.

"Why did you do that?" Brash screamed.

"You're moaning about rights. Well, I have the right to take pictures on a public street," Rosetta said.

"But why did you take my picture?"

"Because you're so beautiful?"

"What are you? A perv?"

"Yes." Rosetta sighed. Snap.

"I should report you to the police."

"That is a very good idea." Rosetta patted the mobile. "Let's *all* go and find some police officers and see what they have to say. OK?" She took a picture of more of the people watching the exchange.

Rosetta's brother, Angelo, would happily have welcomed the clarity of defending a barrier. Sitting instead at Mrs. Wigmore's, he felt no clarity at all about the key question. What did she actually *want* the Lunghi Detective Agency to do for her?

OK, the police had come to her house because the MO of a break-in was similar to the pattern often used by her recidivist husband. But the husband was in jail—apparently justly—and the police were no longer interested in Mrs. Wigmore, so where did a detective agency come in? His prospective client seemed more eager to feed him than to answer that question. Angelo looked at his watch.

"I'm the one who gave it to Des in the first place," Mrs. Wigmore was saying. "So in a way I'm responsible for starting it all off."

"Gave him what?" They were talking about holes in the roof

of Crazy Coffee. How did anybody give someone a hole?

"The cordless drill. It was a birthday present, you see. Top of the range. I *thought* he'd take the hint and put some shelves up for me. It's not women's work, shelves. I wouldn't know where to start."

"But instead of shelves . . . ?"

"He started drilling through roofs. He bought this long bit for the drill first. I suppose I should have wondered then what he was up to, but I just thought it was his enthusiasm. And then he bought a cordless saw to go with the drill." Mrs. Wigmore nibbled on one of the biscuits Angelo had repeatedly refused.

"A cordless drill, and a cordless saw." Angelo wrote the words down more to pass the time than because he needed to.

"Des was always a climber before I gave him the drill. Not that I knew that when he first caught my eye at tango class. No no; what I saw was this handsome, lithe and wiry man who was a good mover. He works at it, mind, does Des. His fitness, I mean. The one thing I believe about his being happy in Langnorton prison is that when he's there he gets all the time he wants to work out. He always comes back really really fit and trim. His body is the envy of many a twenty-year-old in these days of video games and obesity. And I've a friend or two along this street who would swap their couch potatoes for my man, despite his weaknesses and his convictions, and that's the truth. It was like he'd been waiting for cordless power tools all his life. He even bought a belt to hang them from. He thinks of himself as a cowboy, I'm sure he does. So that's what I started off, and all because I wanted a few shelves. So it's my fault and I regret it. More tea?"

Despite the brash girl's challenge, Rosetta and the crow girls did not leave Cobham Court to put the rights and wrongs of their dispute to the police. It was not that Brash backed down—

she struck Rosetta as the kind of girl who wouldn't back down in the face of an oncoming double-decker bus. What ended the confrontation was the shattering explosion of a bottle breaking.

At first no one knew where to look. Rosetta and most of the other people near the barrier started at the sound and looked in all directions to find its source. In that moment it crossed Rosetta's mind that somehow the noise, whatever its cause, was aimed at her and was a form of retaliation from one of the offended crows.

But eventually the cause of the explosive sound was discovered. There were now shards of a beer bottle glistening in the sun in the short lip of Cobham Court between the barrier and Walcot Street.

No one—Rosetta, Brash, Laurence, Smaller-than-the-Others, the other crows—appeared to know where the bottle had come from. They all looked at each other for information but everyone seemed equally at a loss. It levelled the emotional playing field. No one moved.

Which was just as well, because a moment later another bottle crashed in the road near the remains of the first one. This, however, was a jam jar and it made less noise than the beer bottle because it was half-full of red jam.

And now everyone saw the source of the missiles—an open window in the flat above the shop on the corner. The jam jar was soon followed by a yellow tennis ball and three brown envelopes.

David was in despair. Lara had not appeared. And not only had she not appeared, the arrangements they'd made prevented him from going to look for her. Suppose he left his place by the Norwegian furniture store and she arrived? With the crowds— even though they were thinner than at their peak in the early afternoon—he and Lara could miss each other entirely. And if he wasn't there, where he said he'd be, what would she think *then?*

If only he'd got her mobile number. Or an email address. Or arranged to meet her elsewhere in Bath, away from Walcot Street where it was less crowded. If only . . . *If only* . . .

As things stood, David was even worried that Lara *had* come, but not seen him. He'd gone over and over and over the words he'd said, the words they'd shared about the meeting place. There *shouldn't* have been a confusion. He didn't see how she could have gone to a different place. And yet she had not appeared.

How could something as simple as *meeting* somewhere be so difficult? A place was named. There was only one of it. An approximate time had been named. What was so hard?

What was hard was that their plans hadn't taken account of the fact that stuff—*stuff*—sometimes happens. It would have been a simple precaution to say, If something goes wrong, then . . . But he hadn't.

He just hadn't thought things through. He'd been too elated when she said yes. He hadn't even brought one of the agency mobiles with him so he could call home to ask if Lara had, perhaps, rung there and left a message. Why didn't he have his *own* mobile, one that he carried everywhere like all the other kids did? Why was he so stupid as to feel it was better just to borrow one from the family's business equipment now and then so he could spend his own money on other things? False economy, and hubris to boot. It *was* "hubris" to be pleased that he had an advantage other kids didn't, wasn't it? He'd try to remember to look it up when he got home. If he ever *cared* about such trivial things again.

And Lara could perfectly well still turn up, even now. All she'd said was "after three." She never *said* she wouldn't turn up at *five*. David looked at his watch. Or even six. She could even do it and not apologize or explain and David wouldn't be able to fault her. Despite the fact that he had suffered. Had been suffering more with every passing minute since about three-thirty. Suffering so much that even the people running the stall in front of the Norwegian furniture store had noticed him and taken pity.

"You look so sad, young man, and on such a lovely day," a man named Olaf had said to him. "Are you hungry? Here, have some of our delicious Norwegian meatballs."

David *was* hungry and accepted the gift with gratitude. And he smiled and nodded as Olaf explained that Norwegian meatballs, made with ground elk, were far superior to the Swedish meatballs offered at a well-known *Swedish* furniture store.

Elk meatballs would not have been David's first choice for food, welcome as they were. He'd have suggested something Thai from Sukhothai to Lara. Or perhaps Jamaican jerk chicken. He'd found the jerk chicken on his early scouting trip, being offered outside one of the houses on the northern end of the street, not a restaurant. One of those Nation Day surprises.

But elk meatballs it was, and eaten alone. David hadn't even been able to wander up and down the street taking in the novelties and oddities, something he did every Nation Day. And now it was nearly finished, this once-a-year event. Which he had expected to be an all but once-in-a-lifetime event.

Oh sure, there'd been other girls in his life before. Well, one. But no one like Lara. Who was so extraordinary. Beautiful. Clever. Like-minded. The whole package.

Apart from the fact that she had not shown up.

What had happened? Was she lost in the crowds, or confused in her new city? Or delayed by her family somehow? David certainly knew about families and how complicated they could be.

And, true, he *didn't* know what had brought Lara to Bath so near the end of the school year. Most families would have timed a move to allow their talented child to finish school, if the end of term was so close.

There was so much he didn't know about her. So much he *wanted* to learn. Not *just* what those luscious red lips tasted like.

But would he ever get the chance?

Marie was not getting much of a chance to forget what Jason's lips tasted like.

Just as she'd begun to feel annoyed that he was late, just as Cassie took a second look at her watch as if to say, "Is he going to stand you up?" Jason had arrived. He swooped onto the bench beside Marie. And he'd said nothing, not a dicky-bird, about being late. Instead, he'd grabbed her, pulled her close and kissed her full on the mouth. Their first kiss. Right there on George Street. Right there in front of Cassie. When Marie was allowed to come up for air she saw that Cassie's mouth was still open.

"Come on then," Jason said, and pulled Marie to her feet. She barely had time to wave Cassie goodbye. Jason couldn't have made a more satisfying entrance if he'd ridden up on a white charger. Older men were *such* good value.

"Where are we going?" Marie asked, once it was clear they were headed west along the high pavement.

"We're walking," Jason said with exuberance. "It's a wonderful day. We're walking and talking."

"Oh." But then, "Cool."

"It's a *wonderful* time to be alive, Marie, don't you think?"

"Definitely."

"The world's so full of opportunities. All a lively, intelligent bloke has to do is keep his eyes open for them. I can't believe one won't come along soon. I just *feel* it. Don't you *feel* that way sometimes?"

31

Marie couldn't say that she had. But Jason didn't wait for her to find some neutral way to respond to the question. Instead, he just stopped and kissed her.

Then they were on their way again. "There's never been a better time in this country for someone with an entrepreneurial attitude, with networking skills, with ambition. Sometimes I just can't bear that I'm not already halfway to my first million."

"They say the first million's always the hardest," Marie said, to say something.

"Do they?"

"Don't they?"

"I mean, is that something your family says? Like a family saying?"

Marie couldn't remember a single time when the concept of a million, first or otherwise, had been mentioned around the dinner table.

But again Jason didn't wait for her to find a comment. Again he pulled her close and kissed her. And again they set off walking.

"I don't know what starts him off," the beautiful woman from Cobham Court said to Rosetta and Laurence as they sat at a table in The Bell.

"He chucks things out of his window a lot?" Laurence asked. "Would you like some crisps?"

"Thanks, no."

"Er, Rosetta? You?"

Rosetta shook her head as the beautiful woman said, "I haven't been around long enough to know how often it happens but, when it does, it can apparently be at almost any time of the day or night."

"Really?" Laurence said. "Fascinating."

"My flat faces his, though I'm higher up—the building with

the light green door. But sometimes he shouts out the window, this guy, or plays music. Or throws things out. I don't remember bottles before, but I know sometimes he tosses bags of rubbish. And there was a toaster once. And Gloria . . . you remember who I mean?"

"The fierce little old dear who was on the barricades with you?" Rosetta said.

"That's her. Well, she told me that last year he heaved a television set out and smashed the windscreen of a car parked on the street."

"But . . . *why?*"

The beautiful woman shrugged, then said, "You know the lighting shop beneath the tosser's flat?"

Rosetta nodded.

"I don't know the people who run it myself but *Gloria* says that *they* say the guy above them is a Nazi."

"A *what?*"

"She says they hear him through their ceiling, marching back and forth. And . . ." The beautiful woman sipped from her rum. "Ooo, that's good. Thank you, Laurence."

"My great pleasure."

"And Gloria says that the guy's walls are covered with Nazi stuff."

"Swastikas, you mean?" Laurence asked.

"And iron crosses and pictures of Hitler and Mussolini."

"Maybe it's something to do with the trains running on time."

"I don't know, but that's what Gloria says." The beautiful woman shivered. "Is this a double, Laurence?"

"It's just to steady you, after what you've been through."

"Well, I certainly needed something, after the kafuffle. But if I drink all of this, you may have to carry me back upstairs. Still, you're a big enough chap for that."

Laurence seemed stuck for words so Rosetta said, "We'll see

you get home."

"It's flat three, number three." The beautiful woman laughed lightly.

"Kafuffle," Laurence said at last. "Nice word for it. Poetic."

Rosetta said, "How does Gloria know what's on the Nazi's walls?"

"Well, from what I gather, he never locks his flat door. I *know* he never closes his windows because I see them open every day. The sashes are held up by something, a stack of tins, maybe. I just thought it meant whoever was in the flat liked fresh air. I like fresh air myself. Oooo . . ." She fanned herself with her hand. "I think I'm getting tipsy. One drink and it goes to my head."

"Maybe I'd better get you those crisps. Or some nuts?" Laurence rose. "What kind do you like?"

"Cashews, please."

Laurence went to the bar. Rosetta said, "You were explaining how Gloria knows what's on this . . . this Nazi's walls."

"Well, apparently from time to time he stops taking medication of some kind. Then something sets him off. The police get called—like today—and they never have any problem getting into the flat once another building resident opens the front door for them. Gloria may have followed the police in, or talked to other residents. She seems to know *everybody.* I hardly know anybody. I haven't been in my flat for very long, you see. Only . . ." She looked at her watch. ". . . only about a month and a half now." She laughed again.

"So the police have taken this guy in before?"

"They take him in but turn him over to Social Services. Social Services get him back on his pills. Then he goes back to the flat."

"Care in the Community?" Rosetta asked, referring to a budget-cutting philosophy initiated under Margaret Thatcher that closed many British mental health facilities.

"Sounds like it," the beautiful woman said. "Though Gloria also gave me the impression that he has family who get involved, at least to the extent of finding him a good lawyer every time there's an episode. Maybe that's why he never goes to jail."

"It must be awful for you and the other neighbours."

"There are worse things. But city life, eh?" She sipped again. "Even so . . ."

As Laurence returned to his seat he said, "They had salted and dry roasted, so I got you one of each."

"Oh *thank* you. You're sweet."

"Not at all." Laurence turned to Rosetta. "I didn't ask— sorry. Would you like some nuts?"

"Thank you, no."

"So, what were you girls talking about?"

"Tossers," Rosetta said.

The beautiful woman did a bit of a double-take and seemed to see Rosetta with newly appreciative eyes.

"Say what you will," Laurence said. "Adolf and Benito certainly came to our rescue today. Those awful girls were off like a shot when they reckoned we were calling the police."

"Oh, I don't know," the beautiful woman said. "I think Rosetta just about had things under control. Taking pictures was a stroke of genius."

"Do you think?"

"It turned the tables on them, made *them* feel threatened." The beautiful woman faced Rosetta. "I bet if you'd had a few more minutes you'd have had them all combing their hair to make sure they looked good for you."

"Oh, I don't know," Rosetta said, suddenly shy.

"Well done," Laurence said.

"Well, here's to Rosetta." The beautiful woman lifted her glass.

3

"Are they finished at *last?*" Mama asked. She tilted her head to an exaggerated angle to emphasize that she was listening to *silence.*

"Don't count on hearing pins drop for a while yet," Gina said. She was beginning to think about preparing the kitchen table for dinner. Not that she knew who would be eating, or when.

"What about pins?" Mama frowned.

"I'm sure there's more music. And even after the music finishes, I think they have some closing ceremonies."

"To celebrate it's over at last?"

Gina smiled. "You could go out and cheer them as they finish. Take tea for when the people begin dismantling the stage."

"I could do that," Mama agreed. "Or I could make tea for us now. You choose."

"Thank you."

"I should make a pot? What time is it? Where are the children?"

"Angelo will be back." Although he seemed to have been gone for a very long time to talk with this Mrs. Wigmore, even if he did walk. "You and Papa will eat here tonight, Mama, yes?"

"Of course, if he ever comes back with my shopping from his gym."

"He seems so much livelier since he started there."

"I nearly had to drag him in the beginning," Mama said.

"But now it's every day unless it's an earthquake, and longer and longer he stays. Maybe he's found one of those lycra girls." She filled the kettle and turned it on.

"Maybe you should go one day and surprise him. See for yourself what he's up to."

"No no, let him play with the lycra. He needs his dreams."

"Or you could start up there too. Find lycra of your own."

"Now that I like better." But Mama shook her head. "I make a pot of this tea, not cups. They'll be here soon."

"I don't know about the kids or about Rosetta," Gina said.

"*Everybody* would have been here if we'd been allowed to have our Sunday dinner. Why can't this fancy *Day* begin later, after Sunday dinner? What would be lost that's so important they can't start their street at four? Three, even?"

"Suggest it to Rose." Gina wiped down the worktops and mused about what food in the fridge would be easy for people to have, or not, as they pleased, depending on who came back. Maybe she should have sorted food out earlier, but she'd spent the afternoon catching up on paperwork in the office. Rarely was the day so quiet in the Lunghi household as it had been on this noisy Day. Walcot Nation Late Afternoon would just *not* have been long enough.

"My Rose would understand," Mama said. "And maybe she *can* make this committee she joins understand too."

"Have you been out to see what was going on?"

"What would I see that I didn't see from a window?"

"I don't know." Gina took a few containers from the fridge. "People enjoying themselves, up close. Funny costumes. Maybe next year if you can't beat 'em you should go out and dance with them."

"Dancing in my feet?"

Gina smiled. "Exactly."

"I could get Papa out of his gym and into his suit. We could show these street people a thing or two about dancing."

That would be worth seeing, Gina thought as she took fruit from the fridge—it tasted so much better at room temperature.

"If Papa keeps going to the gym. If he feels all this gym work pays off." Mama tried to catch Gina's eye. "A few jobs is all it would take. Small ones, even."

"It's just a matter of when the next case comes along that would be appropriate."

"Just remember, he's still clever, my husband."

"We know, Mama." Gina took out a stack of plates and some cutlery.

"Now all they do is wiggle."

"What?"

"Wiggle. And call it dancing. Back in the village to 'dance' in such a way would get you married." Mama moved toward the door. "I have salad upstairs, with fusilli, for those plates you get out. Shall I bring it down? I'll bring it down." She headed for the landing.

"Thank you," Gina said.

"Does Salvatore come to eat tonight?" Salvatore was the only member of the family who didn't live under the extended roof and his attendance at family meals had been less frequent since Heather and Salvia left.

"I haven't heard from him."

Mama made a face, then left to go upstairs.

Gina put teabags in the pot. Mama would be down again soon, embarrassed that she left before she made the tea she'd promised. But as Gina poured boiling water on the tea leaves, she mused about how lucky she was with her in-laws. Maybe it was not the English way to live under the same roof with them, and maybe not even the Italian way either, especially these days. But same roof or not, there were so many "modern" families that were divided, between the generations. Or between factions. Or between siblings. These Lunghis she'd married into all wanted the best for each other.

The only "issue" in the Lunghi household since Gina first encountered it was Papa's disappointment that Salvatore had chosen to be a painter rather than join the family business like a proper first-born. But Salvatore often worked on cases anyway and, the truth was, father and son were closer now than they'd been in all the years Gina had known the family. Papa had even sat for Salvatore to paint his portrait.

But poor Salvatore. Seemingly settled, after years of—how do you describe it?—"active" bachelorhood? Then to be suddenly, surprisingly, shockingly abandoned by this Heather woman who had engaged and entranced and ensnared him like no woman before her ever had.

Maybe it was the child. Sally had been with Heather for the birth and then for the little girl's first grips and smiles. Had that experience brought out something in him that none of the "models" he brought to family meals in the pre-Heather days had managed? Underneath the anti-commitment exterior was Salvatore really just another Lunghi family man?

If so, it would be a while yet before they found out. Salvatore had been hurt badly. At the meals he attended he put on a cheerful mask but trust, once undermined, is difficult to find again. Gina could tell the wound was still raw, even after nearly six months. She didn't know whether that was visible to anyone else. Mama probably, not that she spoke of it.

Mama was certainly aware that Sally was not bringing women to family meals, which he did regularly before Heather. But she wasn't bugging him about it, although she wanted nothing more than to see him—and Rosetta—settled. Preferably married and surrounded by children, but these days—after Salvatore's false dawn and Rosetta's continued bad luck—Mama would take any kind of pairing that included cohabitation. Let them make a house, the rest will follow. This she did speak of.

Gina considered the evening meal again. Salvatore? Who knew? And David and Marie? Even if one or the other did appear, it would probably be to grab a few mouthfuls of whatever was easiest to refuel with and then run out again. Anyone who could find a way to predict what teenagers will do would make a fortune.

Then Gina heard Mama's footsteps on the stairs coming back down. She got out two mugs for the tea.

Angelo felt relief as he passed through Walcot Nation's border control. It was late in the afternoon now and the collectors were taking donations rather than selling new passports for the few remaining events of the day but today it *was* like coming home after a journey to a foreign land. Even the noise and the crowds felt comforting after a couple of hours of Mrs. Wigmore's excruciatingly slow presentation of her problem. Was it unkind to think that Des Wigmore spent so much time in jail to get away from his wife's chatter? Yes, it was unkind but . . . perhaps Des would volunteer the comment himself when he was interviewed in Langnorton Open Prison about who might have adopted his MO for roof entry. Because at least Angelo's trip had resulted in a new client and a cheque in his pocket.

A little green sticker on Angelo's jacket indicated he was a resident so none of the costumed passport volunteers gave him a second look. But once inside the Republic Angelo gave a second look. He couldn't quite believe his eyes. Was that *David* sitting on the pavement, back against the wall of Norweg, the furniture store, looking for all the world like he was drunk?

Still twenty feet away, Angelo stopped. It *was* David. But the boy wouldn't *be* drunk. Not *David*. He hurried toward his son. However, before he got close enough for conversation, David jumped up. "Dad?"

So, not drunk, but . . . "Is something wrong?"

"Wrong? What could be wrong?"

But something *was* wrong. David never sat in such a slouch. And were those tears welling in his eyes? My God, they were.

Angelo couldn't remember the last time his even-tempered son had *cried*. What was a father supposed to do in such a situation?

But David answered the unasked question by burying his face in Angelo's chest. With his face hidden, he let himself go, sobbing loudly.

Angelo put his arms around his child and gathered him in. "Oh, *David*. It will be all right. It will. It will." But the sobbing continued. Angelo wished Gina were with them, so he could ask her what he should say. What he should do. She always knew immediately, this kind of thing. But all he could think to do was hold his boy tightly, and pat him gently on the back and listen to him cry.

Were there also words that David was saying? There seemed to be words. What were they? Angelo heard, "I thought . . ." Was that it? "What did you think?" Angelo asked.

He felt David tense. Oh God, Angelo thought, did I say something wrong?

But then, as if it were exploding out of him, David wailed, "I thought she *liked* me," and burst into a new bout of tears.

The Old Man was not wearing his resident's sticker. Mama gave it to him before he set out for the gym, but who wants to be stuck? And although the young man wearing a red clown nose only pushed a collection bucket forward, the Old Man said, "I have it here." And he fished around in his gym bag.

The clown was ready to turn away but the Old Man continued to hunt. "Give a minute, give a minute," he said. "Ah. Here." He presented the young man his Italian passport.

The young man looked surprised. Should a clown look surprised? "What's this?"

"My passport."

The clown looked again at the document he held.

"I have a British too." The Old Man began to hunt in his bag again. "Because of all the years I live here. That you would prefer?" Then he saw that the young man had worked out he was being played with.

Clown-for-a-day laughed. He opened the Italian passport and said, "So, tell me, Mr. Lunghi, are you visiting the Republic of Walcot on business or pleasure today?"

David was no longer crying and had pulled away from his father's protection. "So," Angelo said, "shall we go home?"

"*No.*" Then, "Not yet."

After a moment Angelo said, "Let's go to The Bell then. Sit down, gather ourselves."

David stopped rubbing his eyes. "Really?"

Angelo knew why the boy asked. They'd never been to a pub before, just the two of them. "Sure."

Together they walked the length of the street, past the family's doors, negotiating the clumps of crowd lingering for the last of the end-of-Day events. When they got to The Bell, Angelo led the way through the gate that gave access to the courtyard at the back. The area was filled with picnic tables and benches. Father and son waited at one while two men and a woman gathered their possessions and emptied their glasses.

A warren of rooms and spaces opened onto the courtyard behind The Bell. Going with Salvatore to a room that then had table footie had been a big deal for teenage Angelo. Now the grown Angelo wondered how much David had missed out on, not having an older brother. Having an older sister was not the same. Especially not when that sister was Marie.

When the bench was empty they sat. "What would you like to drink?" Angelo asked.

"Vodka and coke. Ice, no lemon." The smile was faint, but at least it was there. David was getting control of himself.

"And if they're out of Smirnoff what would your second choice be?" Angelo asked, his hand on the boy's shoulder.

At that moment Marie was also in a pub, and she really was drinking vodka. Or at least she would be if Jason was served at the bar.

But even if they wouldn't serve him alcohol, Marie wanted *something*. Walking the streets and listening to Jason's plans for fame and fortune was thirsty work. Not that she regretted a word or a minute of it. From that first kiss, full on the mouth in front of Cassie, Marie had felt it was a charmed afternoon.

It's not that Marie hadn't been kissed before, but *those* kisses were more by way of juvenile experimentation to find out what all the fuss was about. *That* kiss and the dozens that followed it were the product of feeling, of passion. Holding her tight, probing her with his tongue, *these* kisses were the real thing. And they were the very first times Jason had kissed her.

From then on the whole afternoon was more like a date than any time Marie had spent with a boy before. Boys and girls in her set didn't "date" like they did in books. They hung out in groups and sometimes wandered off in pairs for awhile, sometimes even for a snog. But this—*this*—well!

For hours—at least it seemed like hours—they had walked and talked. Well, mostly it was Jason who talked but then he'd stop and pull Marie close for kiss after kiss. And Marie liked it. She *really* liked it.

And now, late afternoon, they were together in a pub—not that she'd be bragging about that to anyone later on, except Cassie. Fortunately the Chameleon was nowhere near home or

The Bell, the only pub in Walcot Street. That was because Jason had reasoned that with so many people at Nation Day, businesses elsewhere in Bath would be short of trade. Therefore the pubs would be less likely than usual to be fussy about IDs. Jason always seemed to *understand* things so well, or have theories, even if he didn't always find the simplest way to explain himself.

That *so* differentiated him from the younger, opinionless boys in Marie's life. Some of them might be taller, some even cuter, but they were so obviously boys and Jason was a *man.*

Marie smiled to herself, pleased with what Jason's interest meant about her personal allure. She licked her lips, assessing which lip was the sorer. It was the bottom, but not by much. They both kind of tingled.

When Angelo was finally served at the bar, he bought a packet of crisps along with the drinks. A few shared crisps couldn't spoil an appetite before father and son went home.

He tried to remember if he'd been told when they'd be eating before he left to walk to Mrs. Wigmore's. But he couldn't recall anything being said. He rather hoped the family *would* eat together tonight, what with the usual midday Sunday gathering having been disrupted. There were things about the Wigmore case that would be good to talk about with everyone.

As he returned to the courtyard he saw that David was using a twig to prod a wasp that had landed on the table. No tears, at least. That was something.

He put a glass before his son and then sat. "Apple and melon with ice. And I got some ready-salted."

David opened the crisps, and tore the bag so the crisps could be shared. "Thanks, Dad."

Angelo sipped from his pint of Butcombe. "So."

David didn't look up. He tried his drink and ate two crisps.

"So" what? Was Angelo waiting for his emotionally upset son

to lead the conversation? That couldn't be right. And *then* he came within a whisker of asking whether David had enjoyed Nation Day. But *obviously* David had not enjoyed the day. The upset proved *that*. But what had happened? Angelo sipped some more. "That's good."

Then Angelo began again to try to think of something to talk about. But David saved him. "What was the case you were on, Dad?"

"You heard about that?" Of course he heard. He just said. Stupid. But, "Well, you know Crazy Coffee, around the corner on Saracen Street?"

"Yeah."

"Friday night somebody cut a hole through the roof."

"Cut a *hole?*"

"Drilled four small holes in a square about two feet each side and then connected the dots with a saw. Whoever it was took care not to let the piece of roof fall through. The police found it sitting by the hole Saturday morning."

"Was it robbery?"

Angelo nodded. "Some cash, a mobile, some other small things. Maybe five hundred pounds' worth." According to what the police had told Mrs. Wigmore.

"The thief wouldn't end up with much from that, would he, Dad?"

"Whatever wasn't cash . . . maybe ten or twenty percent of replacement value."

"Isn't that a lot of effort for not very much?"

"You're probably right."

"Unless it was kids, say," David said thoughtfully. "A hundred quid, or a hundred and fifty . . . that would be quite a lot to a kid."

An unbelievable amount to *me* as a kid, Angelo thought, but today maybe a pair of trainers. "But no fortune."

"So . . ." David said, "is Crazy Coffee our client?"

"No. It's a Mrs. Wigmore and she has nothing whatever to do with Crazy Coffee." Angelo smiled. He spread his hands to invite David to speculate further.

Rosetta was, in fact, not far from Angelo and David, although neither she nor they realized it. The Walcot Nation Day Committee operated from a room behind The Bell and now, in addition to the usual armchairs, office machines and long tables, the committee room was host to numerous red buckets.

"OK, OK, please!" Stephanie Slipman was trying to get the attention of the eight other committee members who were present. Although Stephanie was known to harbour ambitions to become committee Chair, she certainly lacked the gravitas and charisma of Barbara Morris, the current Chair. Barbara, however, was not present. "Please!" Stephanie banged a book in the absence of a gavel. "A few of you have never taken part in a count, so I really *do* have to go through the rules."

The red buckets were full of money—from donations as well as the sale of passports. They were "secure" buckets so there were procedures to be followed for opening them and for the counting of their contents.

Rosetta liked accumulations of money, whether it was cash or in a bank account—she did the books for the family business and actually enjoyed the process. So she had always expected to enjoy her first experience of the count. But as Stephanie read through the counting rules, Rosetta found that her sense of anticipation had an unexpected focus.

One of the safety procedures was to put counters into pairs. This was a double protection, both making it less likely that anyone would skim from the piles of cash, and making it less likely that anyone would be falsely accused of doing so. Rosetta's extra interest had to do with who she would be paired to work with. Surprising herself after his behaviour outside the Cobham Court barrier, Rosetta was keen to be paired for bucket-counting with Laurence East.

Whether it was the cogency of Jason's reasoning that the Chameleon needed his business today or the fact that he nearly *was* eighteen and looked it, he had no trouble buying drinks for himself and Marie.

From their corner table Marie watched as Jason smiled and joked with the landlady. Marie had never known anyone with that kind of self-confidence before. Being in his presence made her more confident too.

When he returned to the table, he also brought peanuts. "Food," he said in a mock-caveman voice. "Drink. For woman." He placed the bounty before Marie, a hunter, home from the kill. He grunted.

Marie laughed appreciatively.

Jason slid onto the bench beside her and pressed up close. For a moment Marie thought he was going to kiss her again, but even though he didn't, and sipped from his pint instead of her sweet lips, she felt warm inside. She loved that he was acting like they were a real couple.

Before today she hadn't been at all sure what his feelings for her were. Nor hers for him, if it came to it. She liked him, obviously. And was certainly flattered that someone in Year Thirteen showed an interest in her. But people in her drama class who knew Jason said he was a bit of a gadfly, someone who didn't apply himself, to either his work or his women.

And there *was* that someone—some*thing*—called Jennifer, a busty blonde who swanned around the corridors at school acting for all the world like Jason was her personal possession. Marie had seen Jennifer in action, watched her lean provocatively against the corridor wall while she talked with him, heard her intimate tone of voice.

And Jennifer had even walked past the very first time Marie and Jason talked together after school. She'd touched him on the shoulder and said, "Ooo, Jasie. Trying to make me jealous?"

The incident had triggered Jason to talk about Jennifer. He'd done so positively, swearing that she was nothing to him, and never had been. She'd lived in the house next door all their lives, and because they *had* gone out for a month, back in Year Ten, she thought somehow that gave her rights. But it's not fair to hold a fella's past against him, much less his neighbours. It's not like she'd had his babies or anything. As far as Jason was concerned Jennifer was definitely a goal short of a hat trick and not far off being a stalker. If it got any worse he'd go to a lawyer and get an injunction. He swore he would. She was nothing to him, he said. *Nothing,* hand on heart.

And so Marie, who might have done it anyway, agreed to go out with Jason sometime. No firm plans but they began meeting around the school, once or twice or three times a day. And that's about all it amounted to. Until today.

Today it was *different*. It was like . . . like Jason had *decided* that he wanted them to be a proper, public couple. Marie was aglow. Was this what love was?

Rosetta was not feeling love for Laurence East but she was feeling *something*. She couldn't quite work it out at first. But then she got it. Shockingly, it was jealousy.

Rosetta was *jealous* of the interest that Laurence showed in the pub for the beautiful woman from Cobham Court. She had no *right* to feel jealous. It was not like she and Laurence had ever gone out, or ever spoken of going out, or ever been alone. The most private time they'd spent "together" was walking through the crowds to answer the Cobham Court security call. The second most private time was when they had been in the pub in the company of the beautiful woman. What had she said her name was? Azaria something?

But with or without the right, Rosetta suddenly felt possessive of the huge, reasonably handsome hulk who was Laurence East. Even though she knew next to nothing at all about him. Not what he did for a living. Not where he came from. Not even whether he was single, although he wore no rings.

All that must mean she was attracted to him. Which ought not to have been a *surprise*. After all, one knows that automatically. Doesn't one? But probably it had snuck up on Rosetta because Laurence was so different physically from the other men in her past. Walter, the reptilian already-married lawyer, and Christopher, the narcissistic line-dancing undertaker, were both slight men—well, until Walter put on a gut. The newt and the peacock . . . They were about as unlike Laurence East as they could be.

If they were a newt and a peacock, what was Laurence? Definitely a *bear* of a man. But was he cuddly or was he grizzly?

Only after Marie had emptied her bottle of orange into the vodka glass did it cross her mind that it might not be cool to use all the orange at once. Maybe among regular drinkers it would be taken to mean she needed to dilute the vodka, that she wasn't used to drinking vodka-and-oranges. She wasn't, of course, but she didn't intend to volunteer that information so early in this special relationship. Jason might not yet be of *legal* age to buy alcohol but it was obvious that he drank all the time. You had only to see how comfortable he'd been talking to the landlady when he ordered the drinks.

Jason too was impressed by his talk with the landlady. "Did you see how I did that?" he said with a grin. "How I made sure to distract her so she wouldn't ask about IDs when I ordered the drinks?"

"You did it wonderfully," Marie said.

"People skills," Jason said. "It's the key in the door to business success. It really really is."

Jason was so *positive* about everything he did and everything he talked about. Uncertainties just didn't seem to exist for him. How nice that must be, Marie thought. Maybe it was just something that happened when you were old. Whether it did or not, Jason's certainty provided Marie a guideline for how she should deal with any of her own uncertainties: *decisively*.

So, with her orange-laced vodka there would be no giggly, little-girlie self-consciousness. Picking up her glass, she clinked it with Jason's pint of Stella. "Cheers."

"Cheers, m'dear." Jason drank deeply.

Marie drank too, a bit more at one gulp than she'd intended. It was hard not to choke but she managed.

"You count quickly," Laurence noted as Rosetta finished her share of their first bucket.

Rosetta felt her face flush. Why did it *do* that? "Thanks. I do the books for my family's business," she said, in order to say something. But it was a very stupid something. It implied that her family's business involved cash. "Not that we get paid in cash. At least not very often. I'm just used to counting. Numbers, I mean." Oh *God*.

But Laurence let her slide through the waffle and asked, "What kind of business does your family have?"

"A detective agency."

He paused in his stacking of pound coins. "Really?"

"Walcot Street's finest." What did *that* mean? "My father started the agency years ago. My brother's in charge now, but we're all involved one way or another. The whole family."

"Well, well," Laurence said. "Still waters run deep."

Was he saying she was a still water? He must be. But what

did it mean? And why oh why wouldn't the blood get out of her face and go where it was supposed to? "Am I?" she managed.

"A still water? Oh, I think so, don't you?"

Rosetta knocked over two stacks of fifty pence coins. "And is that . . . good, or bad?"

Laurence smiled, showing his irregular but clean teeth. "Oh good. So many women are shallow and chattery."

"They are? We are?"

"If they're not being vicious, like the girls this afternoon. Whereas you . . . well, *take* this afternoon. You didn't shriek or ask what to do. You formulated a plan by yourself and pulled your mobile out and clicked away until those awful girls stopped what they were doing. That was impressive. Really."

Any blood that had left Rosetta's face made a rapid return. "Someone had to do something. Not . . . not that you wouldn't have handled it too. But it just seemed a good idea at the time."

"And it was," Laurence said.

Jason had his arm around Marie. He was talking about networking. How you just *can't* start doing it too early. How everyone who is anyone says it's the foundation for business success. How there are endless stories of people who met each other in school who went on to work together and make fortunes. How it doesn't really matter if you don't have actual skills. How all you need is a good *idea* and to *know* people who have skills. How a lot of people thought he wasn't serious, but let's see what they have to say when he made his first million.

Marie *loved* that he had his arm around her. Then she realized that he had stopped talking. "So becoming a success is important to you?"

"Absolutely."

"That's good. Great."

There was another pause. Marie looked at her glass, intending to punctuate the exchange by drinking. But the glass was empty. When did *that* happen?

"But I feel so locked in," Jason said then. "So desperate." He withdrew his arm from Marie's shoulder and folded his hands together on the table.

Marie didn't know what was going on. Had she missed something? "Locked into what?"

"The expectation—the *presumption*—that I'm going to university. My parents hardly talk to me about anything else. Everybody at school just assumes that's what I want to do."

"You don't want to go to university?"

"No." Jason finished his own drink. "Well, maybe. But not *now.*"

Marie didn't know what to say. University was a vague future thing in her own life. Expected, yes, but almost never talked about. "Isn't university a good place to network?"

"But I've already *been* networking all my life." Jason waved a hand in short chopping movements. "Think about Bill Gates."

"Er, OK . . ."

"He went off to Harvard, fine. But after a year he dropped out, because he had this *idea*. This *conviction* that it was the right time to follow his dreams. And in my heart, that's what I know too. That it's the right time for me to go into business."

Marie had no clue what factors Jason was balancing, or what was on his mind at all, except that it was no longer very romantic and she had no idea how to get him back on track. "What business?" she asked with a sigh.

Jason turned to her. He took her hand in his.

And there it was again. The warmth, the attention, the focus on her, on *them*.

"I have some ideas," Jason said.

★　★　★　★　★

"How's the apple and melon?" Angelo asked.

"OK. Good. Want a taste?" David offered his glass.

"Thanks." Angelo sipped. Hmm. Could be a lot worse.

David reached for his father's glass.

"What?"

"I get to taste yours too, don't I?"

Well, why not? "Go on. Tell me how you rate it compared to other beers."

David sipped. Then sipped again.

"Enough, enough," Angelo said.

"I had to clear my palette to give the beer a chance."

"And?"

"Hoppy, yet fruity," David said. "I like it."

"I like it too, so mitts off."

"When we go home, can I have some beer?"

Angelo was puzzled. The Lunghis rarely had beer at home.

"Or some wine?" David said. "Either one."

"Where does this come from?"

"To drown my sorrows."

"That's not what beer and wine are for, son. They're to relax, to reward. Sorrows never drown, they always swim."

"Oh."

"Do you want to tell me what's happened?"

David looked at his father, then bit his lower lip. "No."

"Food won't drown sorrows either," Angelo said, "but it can give you energy, and make you stronger and more able to deal with them."

"OK." David took more of the crisps.

"Aren't you hungry? I don't know what your mother has planned for dinner, but . . ."

David seemed to consider. "I could eat."

★ ★ ★ ★ ★

About two-thirds of the way through their buckets, Rosetta too had her mind on dinner. Laurence had eaten a few of the cashews that he bought for the beautiful woman, but a man his size *must* be intending to have a proper meal once the buckets were finished. Might there be a way to contrive things so that they ate together?

"How are you doing?" she asked.

"Fine."

"Not . . . weakening?"

He frowned without looking up from his piles. "Weakening?"

What a silly thing to have said. But maybe she ought to be positive about this. Take action. It had impressed him at Cobham Court. "From lack of food."

"I never eat this early."

But they were still counting money so of course they couldn't eat *now*. "Me neither. I just . . ."

"What?"

"Wondered." She returned to her piles of coins.

Then Rosetta wondered whether plans were being made at home. Nothing had been said but Mama *was* upset this morning because there would be no family meal. So perhaps to compensate, Mama—or Gina—was cooking, even though the Sunday night meal was normally based on leftovers from earlier in the day. If someone *was* cooking, perhaps that good food would impress Laurence.

"I *was* wondering," Laurence said.

He was wondering? The bloody blood raced to Rosetta's face again . . . "What?"

"Just . . . I don't know."

"Go on. What?" Every guest who came to a full Lunghi meal loved the food. She couldn't remember a single one who hadn't. Often as not Mama, Gina and she were urged to consider opening a restaurant.

"OK," Laurence said. "I was wondering what you plan to do with those pictures you took."

Rosetta stopped counting. "With the pictures?"

"You know. Of those girls at the barrier."

"I know which pictures."

"It's just if you're not planning to give them to the police, I would quite like some copies. Or if you give me the memory card from the mobile, I can make the prints myself, if that's easier."

"*You* want pictures? Of those awful teenage *girls* . . . ?" The blood drained rapidly from Rosetta's face.

Angelo and David rose to leave The Bell. But as they stepped away from the table they were suddenly bustled aside by a woman who had run in from Walcot Street.

The woman ran the length of the courtyard, barging and pushing and knocking into tables. With everyone else so mellow, her hurry to be somewhere else was startling. David watched her progress until she turned left and was no longer in sight. Angelo looked behind her to see if someone was in pursuit.

"What's going on, Dad?"

"I have no idea."

"I don't want the pictures for *me*," Laurence said. "For heaven's sake, they're *children*."

Rosetta spread her hands, a family gesture inviting him to continue talking, but when he didn't respond she said, "So in that case . . . ?"

"At the club we post pictures of potential troublemakers."

"What club?"

"Buick's. Down the street."

"The *night*club?"

"I'm in charge of security there. You know—the bouncers, drug control, that kind of thing."

But before Rosetta had a chance to respond, Barbara Morris burst into the committee room. "Stop!" the Nation Day Committee's Chair shouted. "Stop what you're doing!"

"But we haven't finished the count yet," Stephanie Slipman said. "You, better than anyone, Barbara, should know how important it is not to interrupt the count."

"Someone has been *killed.*" Barbara leaned on the nearest table to catch her breath. Piles of coins fell over but then the room went silent. Barbara's voice sounded all the more shrill and desperate. "It's so *awful.*"

Rosetta was not the closest person but she reacted first and went to Barbara's side. "Take your time."

"What *time?*" Barbara wailed. "He's dead. *Dead* in the street. Just lying there. Against a wall. Looking . . . for all the world like all the other drunks . . . but then the blood dripping behind him . . . Oh God. I don't know . . ."

Rosetta wrestled with an easy chair, which stimulated two other people to help get it in a place for Barbara to drop onto. "Someone get her some water, for God's sake. Alan?"

Alan Carter, nearest to the sink, jumped up and found a mug.

Meanwhile, Barbara was saying, "This . . . this *man* . . . He was lying in the street. Simon, the cleaning crew supervisor, he was checking the side streets for when they begin the tidy-up. He just thought the man was drunk. But then he looked closer and saw the blood."

"Take your time," Rosetta said. "What did he do then? Call an ambulance?"

"The St. John's, from up in Chatham Row. And it came, and he was dead, and Simon called me, and someone called the police and . . . Oh God." Barbara sat, shaking her head.

Alan Carter arrived with the water. He handed it to Rosetta, who held it for Barbara. She drank. "Dead," she said. "*Dead.* During Nation Day. That's not what it's all about. We've never had anybody *die* before. Not even from a heart attack."

"You said there was blood," Rosetta said.

"The back of his head. It looked . . . it looked smashed in."

"Was he drunk and fell and hit his head?" Rosetta asked. "Is that what they think happened?"

"The police are . . . they're treating it as . . . as . . . as murder."

"Are . . . are you all right, Marie?"

"Of course I am," Marie said.

"It's just I asked you a question, and you never answered."

"I just did. I said I was all right."

"Before that."

"A question? You did? What question?"

"Whether you want another drink?"

"And what did I say?" Marie was confused about the question stuff but not about not wanting more to drink. She felt awful. The pub felt stuffy. But there was something else too.

"You didn't say anything."

"Oh."

"Are you all right?" Jason asked again.

"Nothing a little . . ." Marie's voice tailed away. Suddenly she pictured the table of steaming, delicious food that the Lunghis always shared on a Sunday. Except not today.

"A little what?"

"I'm hungry. I want to eat something. I think I want to go home."

On hearing the word "murder" several members of the Nation Day Committee broke their silence with a disbelieving gasp.

"You mean the police are treating the death as suspicious until they find out otherwise, don't you, Barbara?" Rosetta said. "They'd have to treat anything like this cautiously but it's not like there's a knife sticking out of his chest."

"They're putting tape around the scene," Barbara said. "They're stopping people in the building he was leaning against from leaving. They're questioning people. It's . . . it's grotesque."

"How old was the dead man?" Rosetta asked.

Barbara shook her head slowly. "Ordinary. Thirties or forties. Oh, I don't know."

"Have they identified him?"

"I don't know."

"Where was the body found?"

"Near the corner."

"Which corner?"

"Where Walcot Street meets Cobham Court."

4

"So *here* you are at last." Mama sat alone at the table as the Old Man came into Gina's kitchen from the landing.

"Where else would I be, but where I am?"

"So long you're gone. Did you get lost in a shop?"

The Old Man unzipped his gym bag and put four bags on the counter. "But you already have so much food here, what good is what I bought?"

"Gina and I don't know how many will eat here tonight. We make sure there's enough."

"I could invite everyone at the gym, there would still be enough."

"So you went to the gym?"

"Of course."

"And spent so much time. Are you getting slower on all these machines you play with?"

"I lift heavier weights now. I'm supposed to lift them *faster?* Huh!" The Old Man took a seat. "Is there tea in that pot? Or am I so late home you drank it all yourself."

"Don't be silly."

"Now I'm *silly?* I thought I was thirsty."

Mama took a mug and then went to the fridge for milk. "For Gina and me we made a pot in case people came home. And now you're home."

"Where is Gina?"

"Checking for messages in the office, Angelo has been gone

so long. You men. You stay out and we worry, but you don't care."

"Worry is your exercise. You could come to the gym instead."

"Of dumbbells I get enough at home."

"Dumbbells are advanced. Not for beginners. Huh!"

Mama was silent as she poured milk into the mug. Then she said, "And what should I do if all the Nation music makes me want to dance?"

The Old Man looked at her.

"I should dance alone in the street? Is that what you want, by staying so long in your gym?" She sloshed the contents of the pot around.

"You and I have danced," the Old Man said with a smile. "We could show them a thing."

They exchanged looks, memories. Mama nodded.

"But none of this Rosetta hippetty-hop dancing," the Old Man said. "Does she still do her hippetty-hop? I don't remember."

"Line dancing," Mama said as she poured tea into the mug. "She stopped that when she stopped her Christopher."

"Ah."

"She can do better, our Rose."

"Than hippitty-hop?" the Old Man asked, but he knew full well that she meant better than Christopher.

At that moment, however, Rosetta's attention was not on improving the quality of her men, although she *was* standing beside Laurence East. Again they were at a barrier on Cobham Court, but this time the barrier was made of blue and white plastic tape instead of metal.

In silence she and Laurence watched as a trolley was loaded into the back of an ambulance. They couldn't see clearly what was on the trolley, but they could guess.

"Are you thinking what I'm thinking?" Rosetta asked.

"Er, what are you thinking?"

"Over there, under the window." She pointed to where a cluster of officers wearing vests marked "police" were taking pictures and interviewing people. "Don't those red tags on the pavement look like they're marking where the body was?"

There was no body outline, but a series of plastic tags and a dark stain made the conjecture seem reasonable to Laurence. "I suppose so."

"And look what they're under."

Laurence looked up.

"It's the same window, Laurence. And it's still open."

"You think the dead guy might have been killed by the mad Nazi throwing something out?"

"*If* those tags do show where the body was . . ."

"Do you think the police know?"

But Rosetta was already waving, trying to attract the attention of an officer. When that didn't work, she slipped beneath the tape.

Marie and Jason entered Walcot Street from the end farther away from the city centre and were not stopped for either passports or contributions because the Day was all but over. That was just as well because Marie was concentrating on trying to hide how unsteady she was. Fortunately, clinging tightly to Jason's arm made this easier. And every time she squeezed his arm, he squeezed hers back.

At first being in the fresh air felt good, a relief after the pub. But the walk home seemed interminable. And although she felt hungry when she visualized food, she felt a bit queasy. That, like not being able to walk properly, was *wrong*. From its wonderful start, the day had gone out of control, and being out of control was not a feeling Marie liked in the slightest.

Jason was saying, "Didn't you tell me your grandfather owns several buildings along here?"

"Did I?"

"When we talked about your family in school a couple of days ago."

"I suppose he does, yes." Marie stopped. "Hang on a sec."

"What?"

"I just want to . . ." She acted as if she needed to make adjustments to her underwear, but the truth was she just wanted a breather. "OK, ready now." Again she took his arm. "I think Grandpa bought some buildings back when they were almost derelict. I think he saved some of them from being torn down. Or something." Though the truth was, Marie rarely listened to her grandfather's stories, unless she was cosying up to him in order to enlist his support for some new project or other.

"Are all the buildings along here? Walcot Street?"

Registering the enthusiasm in Jason's voice left Marie thinking about how he could be enthusiastic about the stupidest things. But she didn't really mind. Not as long as he walked in step with her and let her hold him tight. Maybe that was just the way it was with boys, talking about weird stuff all the time. There was no way she and Cassie would ever talk about which grandparent owned what building. They'd have to be alone on a desert island for their whole lives before their conversations got *that* boring.

But for Jason's sake Marie said, "We live and work in buildings on Walcot Street that he knocked together but I don't really know about the rest. And even the Walcot ones have shops on the ground floor."

"Shops that he rents out?"

"I suppose. Except Grandpa doesn't have much to do with it now. My Auntie Rose handles the financial stuff for everybody."

"Really? Your aunt?"

"Dad's sister. She lives with us."

"How cool."

"Is it?"

"Living altogether like that. One big, happy family."

"I suppose."

"One big, happy, *rich* family."

"What do you mean, 'rich'?"

"Well, the price of property these days . . . all of Bath, but especially in the city centre—and *especially* along Walcot Street."

"What about Walcot Street?"

"Because it's *the* trendy part of town these days."

"It is?"

"Because of all the artists and craftsmen."

Marie was going to ask what artists and craftsmen, but she didn't really want to hear Jason list them. This line of conversation was pushing even her most generous limits of if-he-wants-to-talk-about-it. OK, so the city put up signs calling Walcot Street an "Artisans' Quarter." Surely that stuff was historical and for the tourists. So instead she said, "For all I know Grandpa sold them a long time ago too." Marie stopped again. "But why are you talking about my family?"

"Isn't that where we're heading?"

"Is it?" Marie began to walk again, even more slowly. "Oh, right. For something to eat." Jason was coming home with her . . . Marie's heart beat faster. Her stomach churned more too, but perhaps she *could* manage a bite or two of something. Though she wanted to be steadier before she faced her mother. Or tried to climb the stairs to the kitchen. "No rush, though," she said.

"Besides," Jason said, "I'd really like to have a chance to talk with a successful entrepreneur like your grandfather."

Marie pictured Jason "networking" with her grandfather. Now *that* would be a sight. She laughed.

"What's funny?"

"Just thinking, that's all." Then Marie frowned.

"What?" Jason asked.

"The police cars up there."

"If you wanted me to dance for you," the Old Man said, "you could have rung me at this gym I go to because it was your idea in the first place." He began fishing in his gym bag.

"Was it *my* idea you couldn't climb two flights of stairs without a rest?" Mama said.

But the Old Man didn't respond. He found his passports, which were on top. He held them up for Mama to see. "They call themselves a nation, but do they stamp a passport? They do *not*." Then he found his mobile phone. "Here. See? This I have with me at all times like I live in the twenty-first century."

"I should interrupt and rupture you?" Mama said.

"Huh!"

"Those little phones, who knows what you're doing when they make their noise."

"They take pictures too," the Old Man said. He held the phone up as if sizing up a photograph of her."

"*Stop it.*" She turned away.

"And they play movies, if you want. Make tea too, for all I know, these phones Rosetta has us get for the business." He sipped from his tea.

"Phones should be *real*," Mama said. She went to the doorway that led to the rest of the house and patted the telephone mounted on the wall there. "If *this* rings and I talk, you know where I am, standing here and not twisted into some YMCA pretzel."

The Old Man visualized Mama on a gym mat and twisted into a pretzel.

Mama did not like modern contraptions. And she was suspicious of the way her husband seemed to revel in them. She sometimes felt that he took to all the new devices simply in order to annoy her.

As if to prove her point the Old Man got up from the table and put his mug in the microwave.

"What are you doing?" Mama asked.

"This tea is not so hot."

"I'll make you fresh."

He pushed a button and the machine hummed. "No need."

Mama said nothing but stared fiercely at the back of his head. When he didn't turn to receive her daggers, she said, "Are men put on earth just to annoy women?"

"No no," he said. "We have other jobs too."

It was at that point the Gina came into the kitchen from the office. "Jobs, Papa?"

"Plural with an 's' would be nice, but I'll settle for one."

"How would you like the job of finding a missing person? My husband."

Down the road from The Bell, Angelo and David saw police cars, blue and white tape and uniformed officers. As they watched, two officers opened a gap in the tape to allow an ambulance to pull out of Cobham Court into Walcot Street.

"What's happening, Dad?"

"I don't know."

"Can we go and look?"

Angelo had opinions about people who rubber-necked at crime and accident scenes. The ones who slowed down on the road, for instance, delaying the people behind even more than the accident itself caused. But this was on his home street, down the road from where he lived and worked. And he was out with his son, who not long ago had been crying inconsolably.

"OK," Angelo said. "Let's have a look." As they approached, the ambulance passed them.

"Was someone hurt, Dad?"

"Seems likely, doesn't it?"

"The ambulance wasn't sounding its siren. Does that mean someone's dead?"

It was an interesting deduction on David's part, but Angelo didn't want to encourage morbidity. "Maybe it was called but when it got here they found out no one needed to go to hospital."

Father and son shared a moment of silence. *Could* someone have died? Angelo wondered. Whatever happened, it was unusual to see so many police on Walcot Street.

"Dad," David said, "isn't that Auntie Rose inside the tape talking with one of the policemen?"

"Wow, lots of action," Jason said as he and Marie drew close to the area the police had taped off. "Is it always like this down here?"

"*Down* where?" Marie asked.

"In the city centre."

On both sides of Bath steep hills overlooked the compact centre and most of the city's residents lived on them. Including Jason, with his family. Marie knew roughly where.

"It's not a perpetual hotbed of crime, if that's what you're asking," she said, although drunks *were* known to damage parked cars at night. Walcot was one of Bath's four worst streets for that kind of thing, according to reports in the newspaper.

The ambulance came toward them and, with several other people, Marie and Jason stepped onto the pavement to clear the path.

"Ambulance," Jason said, looking after it.

Well, *duh*, Marie thought. But she was feeling better. "It *can* be pretty lively, especially on weekends. We have a nightclub, you know."

"Buick's, yeah."

"Do you go there?"

"I considered bestowing my patronage once," Jason said, lifting his nose to act the toff, "but I found them to be deuced unreasonable about IDs."

"You mean you tried to talk your way in and it didn't work?"

"Yeah."

Marie *did* like it when Jason put on a voice, a character, instead of droning on about business and his ambitions. "Me too. They're so deuced unreasonable."

Jason laughed and Marie was pleased. She and Cassie once read in a magazine that the way to make men think you were funny was to tell them their own jokes back.

However, instead of trying to extend the toffs-on-the-town conversation, she said, "You know I told you about my Auntie Rose?"

"Who handles everybody's finances."

"She's over there."

Jason looked at the watching crowd outside the police tape.

"That's her, talking to the policeman by the steps of the building near the corner." Marie pointed inside the police perimeter.

"Wow," Jason said. "Do you think she did it?"

"Did what?"

"Whatever the police are here for."

"Don't be stupid." But Marie squeezed Jason's arm to show that she didn't really think he was stupid, just that he was being stupid.

Together they saw Rosetta point to Walcot Street, to the Cobham Court wire barrier, and then to an open window above where she was standing.

"What's the semaphore about?" Jason asked.

"I have no idea," Marie said.

As David and Angelo watched from one direction, and Marie and Jason watched from another, Rosetta opened her handbag. "I took them on my mobile," she told Constable McCough. She opened the phone to show him.

"Oh good," McCough said, but then he did nothing. He didn't ask about it. He didn't try to take it. He just looked.

"The pictures I took are on a card. I have no idea whether anything you can see on them would help, but I'm happy to make them available. Do you want to take the card with you, or shall I call in at the station later tonight, or what?"

McCough considered for a moment. "Let me ask the D.I. Don't go anywhere, Ms. Lunghi."

"I'll be here."

As Constable McCough moved toward a cluster of officers, Rosetta turned back toward where she had left Laurence. But he wasn't there. Had he got fed up of waiting and gone home? But then Rosetta found him. Laurence had moved to the side of Cobham Court opposite to the police activity and he was now standing next to the beautiful woman who lived at number three.

Rosetta was peeved and disappointed and resigned all in one moment.

But then Rosetta felt a pull at her hand. And even before she could respond she felt another hand pushing her away and in a moment she had lost hold of her mobile. "Hey!"

She grasped for the phone as best she could, but it was gone. Then she reached for whoever had taken it, but he was gone too. "Stop thief!" she shouted.

Heads turned toward her call, but Rosetta herself was the

only person who moved. She ran after a man in a black leather jacket who was sprinting away.

5

Mama pointed at the Old Man's plate. "Some more, you'll have?"

"Some more I had already."

"You think I don't know that? Of course I know that. But do you want some more more?"

For a moment the Old Man considered. It was not just his stomach to be taken into account. Mama was upset, because nobody came home this Sunday night to eat after nobody ate this afternoon because of the Nation. Nobody. Not one. So perhaps filling his plate again would occupy her, distract her, please her. "Some more, please," he said. "Just a little."

He watched as his wife angrily heaped more food on his plate. "Not so much, please. A little, I said. What's hard about that?"

"What's hard?" Mama asked, dumping the contents of another serving spoon. "What's *hard?* Making food for nobody to eat, that's what's hard."

"You didn't make. It was already made, these things."

"If I made them before I still made them. But where *are* they all? I ask you."

It wasn't a question. The Old Man turned to his daughter-in-law but he could see that Gina was lost in her own thoughts and not listening. On her plate food was also piled, and not even seconds.

But before the Old Man could think of something that might make Mama feel better, he heard noises from downstairs.

So did Mama. "At last they have come home," she said. "But who?"

The Old Man, Mama and Gina all faced the doorway as they listened to the footsteps mounting the stairs. Gina stood up, assuming it was Angelo.

But it was Salvatore who entered the kitchen. "Hi, guys. Am I too late for a little something to eat?" He looked from his parents to his sister-in-law and back, taking in all the food on the table at the same time. "What?" he said. "I tried to call, but the battery on my phone went dead."

As Rosetta watched the thief in the black jacket bolt across the roundabout where Walcot Street ended, she knew she wasn't going to catch him. She saw him dodge between cars and run up the steep steps that led into Hedgemead Park. Then he disappeared.

There was no point following him. Rosetta wasn't unfit but in the seclusion of the woody park, she wasn't all that sure she'd want to catch up with him anyway. It was, however, a disappointing turn in the events of the day. More than disappointing. She found herself suddenly despondent as she turned back the way she'd come.

But then she saw her brother running toward her. "Where did you spring from?" she asked as Angelo drew near.

"I saw that oik take your mobile."

"You did?"

"You were fiddling with it while you talked to that copper. Then he went away."

"It happened so quickly," Rosetta said.

Angelo took his sister's elbow, to give support. "David and I were on our way home when we saw all the police. Are you all right?"

"Fine."

"Are you sure?" Angelo tilted his head and looked into his sister's eyes.

Rosetta could remember him doing that from her earliest years. Angelo was her big brother far more than Salvatore had ever been. She smiled. "Just pissed off that I let it happen. That's all."

"So which way did he go?"

"Into the park."

Angelo looked across the roundabout. "Ah."

Rosetta could see him consider crossing the street. "There's no point. Come on, let's head back."

Angelo shrugged, which was acquiescence, but as they turned Rosetta caught sight of David running up the street toward them. And behind David was Marie, and even farther back, Laurence and the policeman she'd been talking to. "Good heavens," she said.

"Where have *you* been all this Nation Day?" Mama asked Salvatore.

"Oh yeah, it's Nation Day," Salvatore said. "I forgot about that."

Gina raised an eyebrow, which her brother-in-law caught. She was saying, "Don't pretend you walked through the street to get here without noticing what today was."

Salvatore flickered a smile at her while Mama was saying, "If you forgot about the Nation, why didn't you come for Sunday dinner? Or ring. How hard is it to ring?" Mama patted the kitchen mobile. "You always know where to find us."

"I lost track of time, Ma."

Mama turned to Gina and the Old Man. "My son, the artist. He loses his tracks." But she was smiling. The Old Man was relieved.

Salvatore took a plate and took a spoon from the bowl of

pasta salad. "This OK for me? Not saving it for someone?"

"Eat what you like," the Old Man said.

Salvatore scooped salad onto his plate and then dropped into a chair.

Gina said, "Did you see Angelo out there, by any chance?"

With a forkful of the salad in his mouth, he said, "The first food I've had all day. Mmm. This is yours, Mama? Of course it is. It's great." He turned to Gina. "Angelo? No. Where would I see him?"

"Somewhere. Anywhere."

"You've lost *track* of him?" A glance at his mother. "Careless."

"Some wine you want?" Mama asked. Salvatore nodded so she poured from the bottle into a glass.

Gina said, "He went out to talk to a possible new client and I haven't heard from him since."

Salvatore looked up. "You worried?"

"Not really. It's just it's been a long time."

"I haven't seen him. Sorry. Pass the lasagne, please, will you?"

Gina passed the leftover lasagne.

"OK, that's where Angelo is, or isn't," Salvatore said, "but what about the rest of them? With this food, you could feed an army, yet I'm not seeing any dirty dishes. Nobody's eaten it?"

"He should be a detective, my son," the Old Man said.

"Are you all right, Ms. Lunghi?" Constable McCough said. "I didn't see what happened but one of my colleagues said she saw a man assault you and maybe take something." The officer turned to the rest of the people in the cluster. "Give the lady some room, for God's sake."

"I'm fine," Rosetta said. "He outran me, that's all."

"You were trying to *catch* him?" McCough was clearly surprised.

"Of course. But I never got close."

"What was it he took?"

"My mobile."

More surprise for McCough. "The same phone you were talking to me about?"

"Yes. I was holding it in my hand and then you went to ask someone about it. A moment later it was gone."

"Oh dear. My D.I. wanted to see the pictures you took."

The Old Man, Mama and Gina were watching Salvatore eat spumoni when the door to the street opened. Everyone but Salvatore turned toward the landing at the top of the stairs to see who had come home.

"At last," Mama said.

Gina sipped from her glass of wine.

They all heard a set of feet running up the stairs, followed by another set, much slower. In a moment David burst into the kitchen. "Has anybody called?"

"*Nobody* calls," Mama said. "Not your grandfather, not your uncle, not your father, not nobody. It's as if we're not the twenty-first century."

"I mean a call for me," David said. "Mum?"

"No one called for you or left a message, David. Have you seen—" But as Gina began her question, Angelo walked into the kitchen.

"*There* you are."

"Where else would I be but where I am?" Angelo said. He took in the spread of food on the table. "Great. I'm *absolutely* starving." He picked up a plate.

"Where have you *been,* Angelo Lunghi?"

Angelo stopped. "Gina?"

"Looks like you're in the squits, old bean. What *have* you

been up to?" Salvatore said. "Mama, is there a bit more spumoni?"

On the street outside the family's front door, Marie had hold of both of Jason's hands. "I'm not sure this is a good time for you to come up after all," she said.

"You think I won't make a good impression on your grand-father?"

"It's not that."

"Because I can. I know how to impress old people. I call them 'sir' and give them my full attention and agree with them."

Marie smiled, thinking that her grandfather *would* like all that. It was pretty much the same way she behaved with him when she wanted something. "It's just they'll be talking about Auntie Rose and everything that's happened."

"Ah." Jason nodded.

For a moment Marie wondered if she could get away with bringing him in and their taking food into her bedroom. That would be a wonderful thing to be able to tell Cassie they'd done.

"What?" Jason asked.

It was tempting to try. But everybody eating their food *at* the table was such a big deal for the family that she doubted she'd get away with it. She could just hear her grandmother. "Where is it you're going with your plate when we're all sitting here? And what if you want more?" Plus Jason looked so old. They'd never let them go to her bedroom without endless questions about who he was and what he was to Marie. And then they'd be stuck *forever* with everyone else. No, not a good plan. "I was just thinking how it would be if we went up."

"They won't want strangers around when something so upsetting's happened to your aunt. I can see that. But I *would* like to meet your grandfather and hear about his business

75

philosophy."

"We wouldn't get his attention today. I can just hear him. *'Business is all you can think when your aunt has been assaulted? Huh!'* "

Jason laughed. "Is that really how he talks?"

"I'm a good mimic," Marie said. "They always say that in drama class."

"Your aunt was hardly *assaulted* though." Jason looked back down the street toward Cobham Court where Rosetta had stayed with the police while telling the others to go home, that she would follow when she could.

"I didn't see any of it myself. David just said the man snatched her mobile."

"Not much of a *man*," Jason said.

"To do something like that? I agree." Marie felt a wave of warmth as Jason's presence made her feel protected.

"I mean he's young."

"You saw him?"

"He ran right by us."

"I . . . my attention was on, er, what we were talking about when it happened."

"You weren't talking about all that much. You were tipsy and trying to keep from falling down."

"*No* I wasn't."

"Drinking on an empty stomach does that."

It didn't sound like he minded, so Marie said, "I suppose it does, a bit. And I can just hear my grandmother. *'He gets my Marie tipsy? What kind of a boyfriend does such a thing?'* "

Jason smiled but didn't laugh this time.

"That *is* how she talks," Marie said. "And there could be bombs going off but all she really cares about is who's with who. She's been trying to marry off my Uncle Salvatore for absolute *years*."

"It's just I'm not sure that I'm exactly your boyfriend."

This statement caught Marie by surprise. She dropped Jason's hands. "I don't snog just anybody on public streets, Jason."

"Neither do I."

"Well then."

"It's only . . . well, it just seems a little early-days to give it, like, Facebook status."

Yet he wanted to meet her grandfather. And there was all that talk about the future, even if it was just his future. And all the kissing. What did it all mean? What had it all meant? Marie shook her head, to clear it, to understand better. She *had* been tipsy. She was less than sober now. "*I* didn't tell anybody you were my boyfriend. That was just my grandmother talking, what she would say."

"OK."

And now his tone was so cool. Marie *didn't* understand. If what they had shared today wasn't boyfriend-girlfriend stuff, then what was it? It's not like anybody was talking marriage or children. Though it wouldn't take long for such thoughts to find a place in her grandmother's mind, even though they were so young. She had married grandpa in her teens and look how that worked out.

And now Marie saw that Jason's eyes weren't even on her. Her heart began to race. Could he be about to *break up* with her? That would be *so* unfair, for something that only happened because *he* got *her* tipsy. Why do men have such a struggle facing the consequences of their own actions?

But then Marie felt a tap on her arm. She turned to discover a pale girl, very short, and with a bruise on her cheek. "What?"

"Excuse me," the girl said. "But I'm looking for David Lunghi's house. Aren't you his sister?"

"No," Marie said. "Go away."

"I just thought you'd ring if you were going to be away a long time," Gina said to her husband. "And then when you didn't . . . well, I was a little worried."

"I turned the phone off when I went into Mrs. Wigmore's house. I was there so long that once I got out all I could think of was getting home. But on the way I ran into David and then he and I happened into this business with Rosetta."

"What business with Rosetta?"

"Business?" the Old Man said.

"Some guy stole Auntie Rose's mobile," David said.

"A man *stole*, from my Rosetta?" Mama said. She stood up.

"He didn't hurt her or anything," David said. "He just grabbed the mobile and ran for it. But he was really cheeky because he took it when she was right there talking to the police about the dead body."

"Of course she's David Lunghi's sister," Jason said.

The small, pale girl looked confused. She looked from Jason to Marie and back again.

Marie just wanted the child to go away so she could sort things out with Jason. If he was saying they would *never* be boyfriend and girlfriend . . . but *was* that what he was saying? It was *so* annoying for a complete stranger to interrupt such an important conversation. "Oh *that* David Lunghi," Marie said. "What about him?"

"It's . . . well, I was meant to meet him."

"And he let you down? Well, what can you expect from a . . ." Marie was going to say "from a bloke," but thought better of it with Jason there. "From a geek. He's probably upstairs playing with himself on his computer right now."

"It was me that let him down." The pale girl sucked her lips in for a moment before saying, "Well, sort of. I couldn't help it." She touched the mark on her face and then moved her hand to her mouth as if to signal that she hadn't intended to touch the bruise.

But Marie had no interest in the pale girl's face. She said, "I'm sorry the star-crossed lovers couldn't get it together, but what am *I* supposed to do about it?"

"She obviously wants you to go upstairs and get him," Jason said. He turned to the girl. "What's your name?"

"Lara. But no, please don't interrupt whatever David's doing. And I can't stay. I shouldn't even be here now. I just wanted to leave this for him so he wouldn't think I stood him up on purpose." Lara held out an envelope. "I don't have his email address, see."

"Don't you, like, go to the same school?" Marie said. "Couldn't you see him there tomorrow?"

"You're David's sister, so you'll know how sensitive he is. I don't want him to worry."

Jason took the envelope from Lara and with one of his big, confident smiles he said, "Aren't you nice, Lara. So many people think boys have no feelings, but we do."

"I knew he lived next to the detective agency," Lara said, "and I found the address for that in the phone book. But I still didn't know which side you all live on, and whether it's the one *right* next door or somewhere nearby."

"Trust me, David will get your letter," Jason said. He held the envelope out. "Marie's going to take it up to him *right* now, aren't you, Marie?"

Marie's jaw actually dropped.

"Are you sure you don't want her to tell David you're here so he can come down for a minute?" Jason said.

"No, I've got to go, really," Lara said. "Mum doesn't know I'm out and if she wakes up before I get back, I'm in for it."

"Did she do that to you?" Jason touched the girl's bruised cheek lightly.

"No," Lara said quickly. "It's nothing."

"But you did include your email address in the note, didn't you?"

Lara nodded.

"Good girl. So go on, Marie. Take the note up so Lara knows it's got to David safely. And tell him to email her *tonight*."

Jason's forceful manner meant Marie had no alternative. She tossed her hair and with a little stomp she went into the house.

"*What* dead body?" Gina looked from David to Angelo and back.

"We don't really know that anyone was dead," Angelo said.

"There was an ambulance, Dad," David said. "And when it left there was no siren. And there were red markers on the pavement. And with all those police . . ." He turned to his mother. "The *whole* corner of Cobham Court was blocked off with that tape they use. By the lighting shop, you know?"

"Something certainly happened," Angelo said.

"And it involved Rose?" Salvatore said as he put down his fork.

"She's not hurt?" Mama said. "Tell me she's not hurt."

"She's fine Mama," Angelo said. "Though her mobile *was* stolen."

"Auntie Rose chased after the guy who stole the phone," David said with pride.

"Rosetta *chased?*" Mama said.

"Did she catch?" the Old Man asked.

"No, Grandpa. He ran up into Hedgemead Park. Auntie Rose didn't follow him past the roundabout."

"Perhaps if she went to the gym she could be faster."

"Papa!" Mama said.

"With muscles to subdue and bring to justice. I just said, that's all."

"Don't be so stupid. You *want* Rosetta to run into a park after such a thief? That's probably just what *he* wanted, that bad man." Mama clasped her hands together. "My poor baby, to be the victim of such a thing that you only read about."

Angelo said, "Rose told me that she wouldn't have gone into the park after him anyway, Mama. She's not stupid."

"Now my *son* calls me stupid?" the Old Man said. He looked around the table. "Shall we take a vote?"

"It was your wife who called you stupid, Papa, not Angelo," Salvatore said. "And, face it, she *is* the one who would know."

The Old Man was framing his response when they all heard someone burst into the house and run up the stairs. They turned to the landing door.

"That's probably Rose now," Angelo said. "She's the best one to tell the story."

"I bet it *was* a dead body," David said.

At which point Marie flounced in. She looked from one worried face to the next. "What?"

"Ah, it's Marie," the Old Man said. "Just in time to protect me from all these people who call me stupid."

But Marie was not in the mood to protect anybody from anything. She marched to David's shoulder. "Special delivery, dweek." She flipped the envelope, aiming to land it in his food. She missed and the envelope bounced off the table edge onto David's lap and then to the floor.

As David picked it up Mama rose. "Marie, you should eat. Let me get you a plate."

"I'm not eating, Grandma."

"Of course you eat," the Old Man said. He patted the seat of the empty chair next to him and pulled it out. "A growing girl."

"What *is* this?" David said as he saw his name written on the envelope.

"Traditionally a letter bears the name of the person who is the intended recipient. But you wouldn't know because nobody's ever written you a letter before."

"You wrote me a letter?" David studied the envelope. It was pale grey.

"Not from me, idiot-breath." Marie turned to the table and asked, "Did you know that scientific research has shown that dogs can *smell* people's IQs by their breath?"

"What is this *breath* she says?" the Old Man asked Mama.

"I thought it was dogs being able to smell cancer," Salvatore said. He turned to Gina. "Didn't I read that somewhere?"

"Who is this *letter* from?" David asked Marie.

"Some pasty-faced little alien gave it to me outside the door."

"What?"

"She's about two feet tall and has a complexion like suet."

David stood up, nearly knocking over his chair.

"Don't get apoplexy, you dork's dinner," Marie said. "She said something about she was supposed to meet you but she couldn't face it so she wrote you a Dear John letter instead."

"She's *downstairs?*"

"She said she doesn't want you to come down. Doesn't that tell you something?"

"But she was *here?* Herself? It's not just that you found this on the mat?"

"She was there in miniature person, but by now she's probably been beamed back up to Alpha-beta-taurus or wherever pathetic creatures like her come from."

David ran for the stairs, barging Marie aside.

"Hey, hey, steady on," Angelo said.

"Butthead!" Marie shouted as her brother disappeared down the stairs. But a moment later she followed him.

"Why does Marie run away from this good food?" Mama said, a plate in her hand.

"Do you have *any* idea what that was about?" Gina asked Angelo.

"Who is John?" the Old Man asked. "Why is his letter dear instead of cheap?"

David flung himself out the front door and almost knocked over a bald man whose arm was around a woman as they walked. The man hardly noticed but the woman turned and scowled.

David looked up the street and down the street and across the street, but Lara was nowhere to be seen. He tried to work out where she could have gone.

Unless . . . could this all have been some sort of cruel, wicked, evil joke devised by Marie? He had been careful *not* to say anything in Marie's presence about *meeting* Lara just in case his warped sister took it into her mind to taunt him beforehand or haunt him once Lara got there. But he'd mentioned her name at the table once or twice.

And now it even crossed his mind that maybe the whole thing, including Lara's interest in him, might have been devised by Marie, to repay him for supposed slights she had suffered at his hands. Or as a reality-theatre piece devised by Marie and her drama class friends like that weird Cassie. They probably watched him wait all day for Lara and killed themselves laughing. Or took pictures that would form part of their presentation in class.

The despair that David had felt before the trip to the pub with his father dropped over him again like a heavy blanket.

Marie appeared beside him.

"You are the ugliest, stupidest, most self-centred person in the whole world and you'll never amount to a blot of dogshit," David said, his fury feeding on both disappointment and rage.

But Marie paid no attention to him at all. She was looking around too.

"She's *gone*," David said. "If she was ever here."

"Who cares about *her?* Where the hell is *Jason?*"

"Who?"

"I left him here with the pukey little pus-girl."

"She really *was* here?"

"How else would you get your Dear John letter? No address. No stamp. Duh."

David looked at the envelope in his hand. He tore it open, but then he hesitated. He looked carefully up and down the street again, to be absolutely certain Lara wasn't there. Then he ran back up the stairs, to read his letter in private.

Behind him he heard Marie call out, "Jason? If you're hiding, this is a stupid joke."

As Rosetta neared the family home, she saw her niece standing on the pavement outside the door. At first she thought Marie might be waiting there for her, a silly gesture, however sweet. But just as Rosetta was about to call out, she saw Marie head across the street and then disappear up the steps that led to the Paragon. There was something about Marie's movement and body language that looked wrong, agitated. But Rosetta couldn't follow her niece to find out. She had to deal with the two men trailing behind *her.*

They had stopped too. "Are we there?" Officer McCough asked Laurence. "I mean are we here? I mean, is this where Ms. Lunghi lives?"

"I have no idea," Laurence said.

"Oh. I thought. You aren't . . . ?"

"Aren't what?"

"A couple. You and Ms. Lunghi."

"No," Rosetta said, interrupting. "Laurence and I are not a

couple, although I don't know what business that is of yours."

McCough was embarrassed. "Oh. I just . . . well . . ."

"We're both on the Nation Day organizing committee and I was taking him home for something to eat after all the excitement."

"You were?" Laurence said.

"Was there another reason you came along with Officer McCough and me?"

"I . . . well, I wasn't sure. You know. If I was needed. You know, by him. The officer." He nodded to McCough.

"Needed for what?" Rosetta asked.

"I *was* there. So I'm a witness, I suppose."

"A witness to what?" McCough asked.

"Well, to the original trouble at the barrier, for instance. The teenage girls?"

"Did you see anything that might connect the girls to the death of the unidentified man?"

"Well, no."

"Or anything significant that might not come out on Ms. Lunghi's photographs?"

"No, but I *was* also there when the mobile was stolen."

"Did you see the incident?" McCough asked.

"Well, not as it actually happened."

"You were talking with the woman from number three, Azaria," Rosetta said.

"When?"

"When the man took my mobile."

Laurence thought. "I suppose I was. Now you remind me, she pointed behind me and said, 'That bloke just stole your friend's phone.'"

"So this Azaria did actually see what happened?" McCough said.

"I suppose she did," Laurence said.

"So *she's* the witness."

"But I'm the one who told you about her."

As the two men faced up to each other in a moment of silence, Rosetta sighed. At some other time she might have enjoyed what could have been construed as two men competing to impress her. Instead, what she felt now was fatigue, hunger and diminishing patience. She said, "The Azaria woman lives opposite where the body was found. In flat three of number three, Cobham Court. I don't know her surname but you should be able to find her from that."

McCough made notes. "So she might even be a witness to the murder."

Although the word "murder" had been used before, hearing it from a policeman shocked Rosetta. "Is that what it was? Murder?" she asked.

"The back of the dead man's head was smashed in," McCough said. "We presume we're conducting a murder investigation until it's proved otherwise." He turned to Laurence. "And that, sir, is why the matter of who saw what is so important."

Laurence stood silent.

Rosetta shook her head, fed up with a stupid world in which brash girls intimidated old women and men were murdered during street parties. "If either of you is coming up, then let's do it." She marched to the family's front door and went in.

She heard both men behind her as she climbed the stairs. She was surprised at how much of a racket they made. It didn't improve her mood. Their clatter seemed disrespectful.

So she stopped and faced them. Laurence almost tumbled McCough over. "Do you *have* to make enough noise to wake the dead?" She turned and continued up, grimacing at her own poor choice of words. But to hell with them.

Then, when Rosetta got to the kitchen, she found five members of her family standing with their backs to her. She stopped to take the scene in. Gina, Angelo, Salvatore, Mama and Papa were peering over and around each other into the corridor that led toward the bedrooms. A chair was lying on the floor. She heard David's name but nothing more of the whispered conversation. Had the whole world gone loopy? "Excuse me," Rosetta said. "Is anybody home?"

The five Lunghis turned together as if choreographed. Salvatore said, "Sis! You're all right."

"Why wouldn't I be? *What* is going on?" She stepped in. The two men followed.

McCough was first, drawing everyone's attention because of his uniform. Then Laurence followed, stooping under the doorjamb. Rosetta saw her mother's eyes widen as she took in the sheer *size* of the man. For once, the family kitchen seemed too small.

Marie had *never* felt smaller. How *dare* Jason not wait for her to return from the errand *he* had forced her to do? His bullying about David's poxy letter was bad enough—something she might even break up with him over. But how was she supposed to make him beg not to be ditched if he wasn't there to be confronted? It was *very* aggravating.

And humiliating.

She pulled out her mobile and rang his number, ready to tear a strip off him for leaving her alone. But instead of getting through to him she was put straight through to his voicemail, so his phone was off. He had turned it off when they were together in the Chameleon and must not have turned it on again.

She almost left a message, but then hung up instead so she could make sure that what she said was right.

So where *was* he? She hadn't been gone long enough for him to have got far. Even though there were still a lot of people in the street, and the crew had begun dismantling the main stage, she still had pretty good views in both directions. But he wasn't in sight.

She *had* told him it wasn't a good day for him to come into her house and meet the family. So is *that* what had happened? Had he thought she wasn't going to come back down after giving the letter to David? Granted, she hadn't said specifically "I'll be back down in a minute," but *honestly.*

So where would he have gone? Home? To do that he'd have crossed the street and climbed the steps that led to the Paragon and London Road. Which *would* also explain why she didn't see him along the street.

So that's where Marie went.

As she climbed, she considered again whether it was *really* possible that Jason had thought she wouldn't come down even to say good-bye. Especially when they'd been in the middle of an important conversation about whether he was going to be her boyfriend or not.

Or was *that* the key? That he didn't *want* to continue the discussion and he had just used the opportunity to evade it.

Wouldn't that be just like a man!

The thought made Marie even angrier. She was going to give the snivelling coward what-for when she found him. If she was right about where he'd gone she might even catch up with him now. How long had she been in the house?

At the top of the steps Marie crossed the busy road and went up Hay Hill, a little cut that connected to Lansdown Road. If Jason *was* on his way home, that's where his nearest bus stop was, on the corner of Alfred Street. His parents' house was way up the hill. He'd talked about taking the bus.

But, when she got to the top of Hay Hill, she saw that neither Jason nor anybody else was waiting across the street at the bus stop. That *could* mean a bus had just come, but when she looked up the hill she couldn't see one. Which needn't prove anything, and yet . . .

Marie crossed to the stop and stood there, half waiting for the next bus and half recovering from the climb she'd just made. It was always *possible* Jason would appear from somewhere. There *was* a pub a few doors along on Alfred Street.

Again she went over everything that had happened during the day, from the big kiss on her mouth when he arrived late all the way to his sending her upstairs with the letter from David's little wad of bruised dough. But she couldn't make sense out of it. She couldn't work out how it could lead to his disappearing so abruptly.

Marie felt angry and confused and puzzled, all mixed up together.

David's feelings were mixed up too as he lay on his bed, having first wedged his door closed with a chair to prevent anyone—especially Devil-girl Marie—from intruding on his privacy.

He needed to be alone and safe to savour the fact that Lara had come to his house. And, she had *written* to him.

Which was good, wasn't it? Meaning that she liked him and wanted to be his friend? Maybe even his girlfriend?

Yet she hadn't stayed to say hello or explain anything.

So was it all, in fact, bad? Was it her way of letting him know that she didn't want to know him anymore, however friendly she'd been since she arrived at school. That she'd come to her senses and realized that, being beautiful and clever, she could do better. Was it, in fact, a Dear David letter?

David feared to read what she had written without steeling himself to face the worst. But what could the worst be? It could hardly be a *real* break-up letter because they had never been a couple or going out. But if it *did* contain bad news, it would still feel that way to him. Because it would mean the loss of his hopes. His dreams.

Not that David was totally inexperienced with girls. Even kissing them. Well, one, and one who was older than he was at that. But that's not to say he felt comfortable around them. So even if the letter was good news, how would he cope and know what to do?

David's heart was pounding when he finally slipped a sheet of light grey paper out of the light grey envelope.

"Take a seat, Laurence, please," Rosetta said. She turned to her mother. "This is Laurence East, Mama. Give him some food while I'm in my office, will you? I'm sure he's hungry." To Laurence. "You are hungry, aren't you?"

"Well . . ."

"There's enough, isn't there, Mama?"

"Oh yes. Plenty." Mama jumped up.

"Officer McCough and I will be back out as soon as we can." Rosetta beckoned to the policeman and headed down the corridor the family-five had just been peering into.

After a moment, McCough followed.

Which left the Lunghis alone with Laurence. For seconds they looked each other over in silence.

Then things began to happen. Mama got a plate. Salvatore cleared his throat, seeming to prepare himself to say something. But it was the Old Man who spoke first. "A policeman Rosetta brings into the house?" He looked around the members of his family. "Who knows about this?" Then he fixed Laurence. "You, big mister Laurence East? Are you a policeman too?"

"No, no."

"Well, what do you know about that one who is?"

With five pairs of Lunghi eyes concentrated on him, Laurence said, "Er, not much."

"Why does my daughter bring a policeman into this house?"

The Old Man turned to the rest of the table with his arms out. "This is what we want to know, isn't it? Or am I stupid again?"

"It's what we want to know, Papa," Salvatore said. "Along with who this Laurence East is." His scrutiny of the big man at their table was not a friendly one.

"I don't know exactly what the copper wants here." When this response was greeted with silence, Laurence said, "Look . . . maybe I should just go." He pushed his chair back from the table.

"Why would you go?" the Old Man asked. He appealed to the others. "Why would this Laurence East want to go when Rose said he should eat? I may be stupid, but isn't this suspicious?"

"Hang on," Laurence said.

Mama said, "Would you like some lasagne, Mr. East? It's only cold but very delicious. It was our Rose who made it."

"Look, I'm just on the committee with Rosetta. Organizing Nation Day."

"*You* did this?" Mama said.

"Did what?"

"Decided to start at such a time that we couldn't have our family dinner?"

Laurence glanced at the doorway to the stairs, clearly estimating how easily he could get out if he ran for it. But it was Gina who defused the situation. "Please, Mr. East, have something to eat. I'm sure Rose won't be long. And meanwhile, why don't you tell us how today went from the organizers' point of view. Is this your first year on the committee too?" She took the plate from Mama. "If you don't fancy cold lasagne, how about some of the pasta salad?"

The first surprise was that Lara's message was handwritten. What could *that* mean for such a computer-literate person?

"Dear David," it began, "Sorry about the scrawl, but I can't turn the computer on without waking Mum up and that's more than my life is worth. I just couldn't make it this afternoon. Mum was sposed to go for a visit and I would have stayed home 'studying'—which I really need to do from being at a new school now—but I would have met you instead. But she didn't go out cause there was some kind of dispute where she was going to. I told her I wanted to go out for a walk anyway because of the nice day but she got mad because of being left alone—it's a new place for her too. And she also wanted me to do some stuff around the flat while she had a headache on the couch, so I just couldn't meet you. I don't have your email address or mobile number because I was too shy to ask, even though I'm sure you wouldn't have teased me for asking or anything. It's just . . . well, you've been so great at understanding how hard it is for me to come here to a new school like this, I didn't want to leave you hanging. I just couldn't do anything to let you know. I even tried to get a number by looking up the detective agency in the phone book but when I called it was only a business message and I don't know if you get into trouble when people leave personal messages for you there. I didn't want to take the chance. My mum would go crazy if she had to give me messages. Good thing she doesn't know anything about computers. And today isn't a business day anyway so probably you wouldn't get it before tomorrow anyway. But I'm really really sorry. I would have loved to walk on the street and use my passport because I don't have a real one. I hope you had a good time anyway. Probably better without showing a newcomer around and making sure she didn't get lost. See you in school tomorrow. Or outside a bit early if you don't hate me. x Lara cyberlara@windylake.co.uk"

David read it all again. And then again. Especially the end. The "x." There was no other way to interpret the letter than as friendly. There was no other way to interpret the "x" than as a kiss!

Angelo said, "You can understand that a policeman arriving at the house is not the kind of thing that happens every day."

Laurence nodded. "I daresay."

Gina was heaping food onto the plate. He *was* a big man, after all. She said, "You had wonderful weather for the event."

Angelo glanced at his wife and took the hint that the subject should change to neutral things. Perhaps that *was* best until Rosetta came back out to explain.

Salvatore, however, took no hints. He said, "Look, pal, you must know a little bit about why the copper's here. Is Rose being accused of something?"

"No, no. It's a witness thing. And also because her mobile phone was stolen." Laurence accepted the brimming plate from Gina. "This looks great." He spread a paper napkin on his lap.

Mama said, "It's make-do. *Usually*, on a Sunday, we eat lunch *together*. Like a family."

"Uh huh," Laurence said, his mouth now full.

"The telephone thief we already heard about," the Old Man said. "And that Rose chased this thief and didn't catch him and should maybe start at the gym for speed and muscle."

Salvatore said, "So *is* all this about the theft of her mobile?"

"Only in part." Laurence turned to the women. "This pasta salad is delicious."

"What *part?*" Salvatore said.

"There may be something on the pictures she took."

"Hang on, hang on. What pictures?"

"With her mobile. She took pictures at some trouble we had earlier in the day."

"Either the mobile was stolen or it wasn't."

"It was."

"So how can the copper be in there because of what might be on the pictures?"

"I'd just taken the memory card with the pictures out of the phone," Rosetta said, showing it to McCough. "In case your D.I. wanted to take it back to Manvers Street for a closer look. You went to ask him. Do you remember?"

McCough gave a little snort. "All D.I. Phillips said was, 'Depends what's on the pictures.' As if I couldn't work that out for myself. I was going to come back to ask."

"Well, we won't know till we look, will we? Not that I was aiming to snap anything more than the awful girls. And all that *was* before the poor man was killed. Do you know when it happened?"

"I don't, no."

Rosetta put the card into a reader and tapped some keys.

McCough looked around the room. "This is quite a place you've got here. All this equipment. What's it for?"

"As well as the agency's accounts office, this room is our equipment store." Tap tap.

"What agency?"

"The Lunghi Detective Agency. It's the family's business." Tap tap.

"Really?"

Rosetta glanced at McCough because of a tone in his voice. "Is that a problem of some kind?"

"Not . . . well, it's just I thought you might be joking me."

Rosetta turned away from the computer to face the man. "*Joke?* Why on earth would I do that?"

"I get teased a lot and mostly I don't know when it's happening."

Rosetta tried to absorb the significance of what McCough was saying, but then a "ping" from the computer brought her attention back to the screen. Tap tap.

McCough said, "I try my hardest to be careful and do things the way everybody wants me to, but that doesn't make it any better."

"Oh." Tap tap tap.

"When I ask them at the station why they do it, they say it's because I'm new here. But I don't think that's true, because it always used to happen before, too. My mum always told me I wasn't the brightest shine on the penny, so maybe it's that."

Rosetta decided that she was being told this policeman was bullied by his peers, but then the first of the pictures she'd taken at Cobham Court came up on the screen. It was the face of a fierce young woman.

"Ooo that's not a very ladylike expression she has there," McCough said.

"I think we're more interested in the people in the background, aren't we?"

"Right. Right."

Rosetta clicked through some pictures. "Like who that guy in the reddish jacket might be?"

"I assume the police officer's here for something to do with the murder," Laurence said.

"*Murder?*" Angelo said. For them all.

"But honestly, I don't know much about it."

"A murder case? My Rosetta?" the Old Man said.

Gina said, "Please, Mr. East, tell us what you *do* know."

"Well, Rosetta and I were in the Nation Day office counting money," Laurence began, and he went through the story, including an account of how Rosetta had come to take photographs in Cobham Court. "Then, on the walk here, the police officer who's in there with her now said that they're treating it as a murder case because the back of the dead man's head was 'smashed in.' "

Mama said, "My Rosetta is mixed up in a smashed in?"

"It can be smashed and not a murder," the Old Man said.

"The guy's unlikely to have cracked open his own head, Papa," Salvatore said.

"*Things* can smash heads."

"Without a person attached to them? Like what?"

"Or a fall can smash heads. This dead man might have been on a roof, like so many along the street today." The Old Man turned to the others. "People come out on roofs and balconies to watch today. He could fall. Am I wrong?"

Angelo said, "You're not wrong, Papa. But a fall would be likely to smash other bits too."

"Who said it didn't? Did this big Laurence say it didn't?"

Laurence said, "Honestly, I just don't know. I suppose they have to think the worst until they know for sure." He turned to Mama. "Delicious . . . what do you call this?"

"Ziti," Mama said.

"You should open a restaurant. You really should."

Looks were exchanged between the Lunghis, because Mama had just freed herself from an unfortunate involvement in a restaurant, though participating as an investor rather than as a cook. "Thank you," Mama said. "I'm glad you like."

Salvatore said, "Have they identified the dead man?"

"Not as far as *I* know," Laurence said. Then, again to Mama, "And the leaf in the salad that has a lovely peppery taste. What is it?"

"That will be the arugula," Mama said. She was taking to this giant of a man. But such enormous babies he would make. No fun, a big baby. Still these days the girls all had Caesar sections so maybe it wouldn't be so bad.

"We call it rocket here," Gina said.

"We do?" Laurence looked at his plate. "Well, everything I've tasted is delicious. Really."

"The policeman," the Old Man said. "Him with Rosetta, we could ask about the smash and the identification."

And as if on cue, McCough and Rosetta returned to the kitchen.

"Ask what, Papa?" Rosetta said.

"Who is this smashed head? And did he have other smashed things too? Arms or legs. Or . . ." getting a new idea, "or was there something underneath him that he fell on? Because if this dead man fell from the roof he could have fallen on something except for smashing his head." The Old Man faced McCough. "So?"

"Er, I'm not sure I know about any of that, sir," McCough said.

"Nor whether the dead man has been identified?" Gina said.

"Not that I know about," McCough said.

"So what *do* you know?" Salvatore asked.

"That the victim was wearing a reddish jacket and that Ms. Lunghi here seems to have taken a couple of pictures of him."

"Rose?" Gina said.

"There is a man in a maroon jacket in the background of a couple of the pictures I took." Rosetta held up two prints she'd made and then passed them to Laurence. "Did you notice the guy?"

Laurence put down his fork and held the prints with both hands. He studied the top one, then the other one. Then the top one again.

"They're pretty blurry because he was in the background," Rosetta said.

"It's that beard," Laurence said. "It *is* a beard, isn't it? Not something smudgy from the printer?"

"It's a beard. One without a moustache. Like a mullah," Rosetta said.

"I think I may have seen this guy," Laurence said.

"At Cobham Court?"

"Not there."

Everyone watched as Laurence looked at the two prints again.

"Then where?" Rosetta asked.

"It would have been from the club." Laurence screwed his face up in thought. "Yeah, I'm pretty certain. Once, maybe twice in the last week."

"What club?" McCough asked.

"I work at Buick's."

"The nightclub?" Salvatore said.

"I'm in charge of security there." Laurence looked again at the second picture. "I encourage my guys to remember faces. And we certainly had a guy with a beard like that come in recently."

McCough said, "I'm going to have to ask you to come to the station with me and Ms. Lunghi, Mister . . . Did I ever get your name?" McCough took out his notebook.

"Laurence East. So, does this mean I'm a witness after all?"

6

Marie stood at the bus stop for what felt like a long time as she tried to decide the best thing for her to do next.

She *could* go to Jason's house. She had his address—it was on his business card. How *cool* was it still to be in school and have a *business* card? Well, Marie wasn't quite sure whether it was cool or not but it *was* part of the Jason package and *he* had certainly impressed her. Until a few minutes ago. Could it have been as little as half an hour since he'd bullied her and then vanished?

So, she had the address and knew it was up Lansdown Hill. Probably a bus driver could pin down where it was best to get off. And then she could ask people there for more directions. Yes, she was confident she could get to Jason's house.

But was going to his house the best course of action? What would she actually *do* there? Ring the bell and . . . what? Ask whoever answered if Jason was home? Turn around and look a fool if he wasn't? March in past his parents or little sister and say she'd wait for him? Oooo, no, not *that*. And what if he *was* at home. Wouldn't she look a fool anyway if he came to the door and acted charming in the face of her anger?

The problem with going to the house was that it was *his* territory rather than hers. And that wasn't even taking account of the neighbour girl, Jennifer, who had the puzzling proprietorial attitude to him. And what if Marie was to run into *her*? Ew. No, going to Jason's wasn't safe, wasn't right. Which was useful to have worked out, especially just as a bus crossed George Street and headed her way. Marie retreated from the bus stop and headed down Alfred Street.

There she came to The Assembly Inn and it occurred to her that the *best* thing to do would be to send Jason a really *stinging* text message, and then go to her own home. But to work out exactly what to say to him would need some thought, some time and space. If she went home to do it, who could tell what she'd walk into the middle of.

For a moment Marie even conjured dreary little David getting up to disgusting things on the kitchen table with the pasty little smudge of a girl who'd left the letter. Ugh. Much better to settle herself in a pub and work it all out there.

David was still in his room. Unlike his sister, he'd been certain for some time what he wanted to do next, which was to email Lara. But like Marie, he wanted the words to be just right. And he was finding it a struggle.

One tempting possibility was to send, "Dear Lara, thanks for your letter. Will you have my babies?"

When he had the thought, it made him giggle. For a while he even tried to convince himself that it *was* the right message to send, being short and funny. David's one previous success with a woman was because she thought he was funny. Wasn't it right to play to one's strengths?

But would Lara find it funny? He went back and read her letter yet again. There wasn't anything in it that seemed humorous. Yet at school, as he'd shown her around, she did laugh at all his jokes. And sometimes when he didn't even know he was making one. But in the end David instantly abandoned the plan when it occurred to him that Lara's mother might monitor her mail. Definitely not an email to send to someone who might have to explain it to her mother. But if no babies, then what?

"Dear Lara, I suffered all day long but your letter makes it all better . . ."? Honest, but lacking in style.

"Dear Lara, I can't express what a joy and a relief it is that you risked your mother's wrath to come to my house to leave a message that asks me not to hate you . . . How could I ever hate a woman who would do all that to make me feel better? There couldn't possibly be a better woman than you. Please have my babies. Or at least snog me at break-time."

David was chuckling to himself when someone knocked at his door. He jumped up from his seat. The sound felt like a cannon shot, an earthquake, an explosion. He'd been so deep in the world of Lara that he'd completely forgotten there was any other.

The knock was repeated. "David?"

It was his mother. At least it wasn't the repulsive Marie.

"David, open the door please."

He hid Lara's letter under his keyboard and minimized his email screen. Then he moved the chair away from the handle and opened the door. "What?" he said. Then realized the word by itself sounded stark. And rude. "Mum."

"You haven't eaten and we're about to put the food away. Do you want to come to the kitchen and make up a plate?"

He was about to say no when he said, "Yes, please," instead.

The Assembly Inn was busy but not full. Marie spotted a small table by the windows in the front, beneath a big TV screen used for sports. There was something sporty on it now—bats and balls—although the sound was off. The position was ideal. She could be on her own but also have a view of the street in case Jason walked by. She was pleased with her plan and looked forward to a few minutes producing the perfect text. Perhaps over a vodka and orange? How appropriate would *that* be?

At the bar, however, she could just *tell* that the barman would ask for ID if she tried to buy alcohol so instead she ordered an Appletise. Then, glass and bottle in hand, she headed for her table. But just as she got there a man seemed to come from nowhere to beat her to it.

"Ex*cuse* me," Marie said in exasperation. "But this table's mine."

The man was in his late twenties, with dark, thinning hair. He looked at the two empty chairs. "I don't see a bag or a jacket or anything." When he spoke, the only part of his mouth that moved was on the right side. But his brown eyes were warm and his tone was friendly enough. And he hadn't said anything sarky like that he didn't see a "reserved" sign.

So Marie took a breath and came clean. "OK, I wasn't sitting there yet, but if I'd thought someone else was going to take it, I would have left something before I got my drink."

The guy gestured with the hand that wasn't holding his drink, a kind of shrug. "We could share. Two chairs . . . and there seems to be plenty of room."

Marie looked at the table. She looked at the man. Well, what harm? "Yeah, OK. But I've got something I'm working on."

"And I can see you're keeping your head clear for it," nodding to her Appletise. "I promise I won't tap my fingers on the table or spill, or even look over your shoulder to see who's passing by." He put down his pint and pulled a chair out for himself.

Marie put her things down too.

"I'm Rob." He put out a hand.

"Marie." And she sat. It felt good to sit. She could still feel the climbing she'd done on the steep stairs.

"And are you a student, Marie?"

"Uh huh." Marie took a small notebook out of her handbag, and then a pen.

"At Bath or Bath Spa?"

Marie almost laughed at the idea he thought she was old

enough to be at university, but she restrained herself. Rob was not *bad* looking and was dressed well, if conservatively, in a sports jacket. If Jason *did* pass by, or even come into the Assembly before going home, it would be *too* perfect if he found Marie sitting there with another man. An *older* older man. So instead of revealing her age Marie said, "Bath." Well, she was a student *in* Bath, if not *at* Bath.

"Impressive," Rob said. "And there's so much going on up there."

"Isn't there just." Marie *had* been up the hill on the south side of the city to Bath University. She wasn't actually all that sure where Bath Spa University College was.

"What are you reading?"

"Drama."

"Cool. With all the sciences up there I didn't know they had a department."

"It's small," Marie said, "but select."

"Well, here's to drama," Rob said. "The world would be a poorer place without it." He tapped his glass against Marie's and sipped.

There was a kind of mannerliness about this man that pleased her. Was that how men became when they were even more mature than Jason? She lifted her glass and tapped his back, having just about decided that the talking out of the side of his mouth thing was kind of cute. She sipped from her Appletise.

In the living room Angelo, Salvatore, Mama and the Old Man sat around a coffee table. On it were six wine glasses—five full—and two wine bottles—one empty. Gina came in from the kitchen and joined her husband on the settee.

"How is David?" Angelo asked.

"He seems completely normal now. He put together a big plate and took it back to his room." She picked up her glass and drank. "Oh, that's good. What a day."

"To knock a chair over! Why did David act in such a way?" Mama said. She too sipped from her wine.

"Perhaps the boy is on drugs like so many we read about," the Old Man said with a sigh. "Such a world it is today."

"Such a thing to say," Mama said.

"I can't say a *perhaps?* It's not a *he-is.* How would I know that?"

"David's problem is a woman," Angelo said.

The others turned to him.

"Ah, the boy looks up to his uncle," Salvatore said. "Tell us more, bro."

"A girl from his school was supposed to meet him on the street this afternoon but she didn't show up. He waited for hours and was more upset than I've ever seen him."

"When did you find out about all this?" Gina asked.

"I ran into him on my way home from Mrs. Wigmore. He . . . don't tell him I told you, but he even cried."

"Why didn't you tell me? *Honestly.* First you're away all day without a call and now this. I certainly haven't trained you properly."

"And then they slide back from the training," Mama said. "You teach an alphabet and they never remember past C."

"When was I supposed to tell you?" Angelo said. "I wasn't going to announce it while we were sitting around the table and then everything got overtaken by this murder stuff."

"A smashed head still doesn't have to be a murder," the Old Man said.

"We know, Papa," Angelo said.

"I'm just saying. Now Norman Stiles, that *was* a murder. A knife and no doubt."

A groan came simultaneously from the siblings. Even Mama joined in after a moment. Only one murder case had ever come the way of the Lunghi Detective Agency and if the Old Man was awake he was ready to recount it, from the first visit to the office by the murdered man's son to his own discovery of the critical piece of evidence. Every Lunghi had heard the story countless times.

"What?" the Old Man said.

"We don't have this smashed-head as a case, Papa," Salvatore said. "What we do have is Rosetta." He looked to the others. "Is there anything we should be doing to support her?"

"She seemed to have things pretty much under control," Gina said. "And with *two* men," Mama said, "including such a nice big one."

"Get a life, Mama," Salvatore said. "Rose isn't interested in either of those guys."

"What makes you such an expert? You who never introduce your sister to your friends."

"I didn't realize Rose was into women. But if you think she might be batting for the other side these days . . ."

"Batting?" Mama looked around. "What is this batting now?"

"It's cricket," the Old Man said. "Maybe Rosetta takes it up so she can become fitter and catch a thief next time." But then he turned to address Salvatore. "Tell me, whatever happened to that woman with the baby that wasn't yours? I don't see her anymore."

There was a sudden silence. This was the question nobody asked Salvatore now.

"What?" the Old Man said, looking around the room.

"Just hush, all right?" Mama said.

Gina said, "When Rose gets back we can ask if there's any way we can help. It must be horrible for her." Rosetta had gone with McCough and Laurence to the police station.

But the Old Man was not put off. "It's hush now? I want to know about my son's woman and her baby that turned his world

105

upside down. Why is that a hush?"

Quietly Salvatore said, "Heather and Salvia aren't in Bath anymore, Papa."

"I *told* you all of this," Mama said to her husband.

"We don't see each other now, Papa."

"But you were so much together," the Old Man said. "When did such a thing happen?"

"Months ago."

"I *told* you all of this," Mama said again. "Why can't you pay attention? Attention is just an A."

"Months ago is plenty of time to forget. So I forgot. It's a crime?" He lifted a glass. "So what else was there I forgot? That she found another man?"

He drank while the others watched.

Marie drank from her glass and then emptied her Appletise bottle over the ice cubes that remained. She *ought* to be composing a pithy, stinging text message for Jason. But she was enjoying Rob's flattering attention too much. Anyway, maybe it would be better just to blank Jason, as if she didn't care.

"So will your drama course lead to a career as an actress, or a dramatist, or a director or what?" Rob asked.

"Or all of the above," Marie said lightly. "Although I'm thinking I may take a year off before completing my degree." Before starting it *was* before completing it, so it wasn't a lie. "Maybe get a job."

"Jobs are good. More experience of the world plus a bit of money."

"Or even start a business."

"A business . . . wow. That's ambitious."

"You don't get anywhere without ambition, or determination," Marie said. "Or networking."

"What kind of business do you have it in mind to start?"

"Something with words. With creativity."

"Using your dramatic training. Good thinking. Do you have something particular in mind?"

"I'd really rather not say."

"Very wise, very wise. I might steal it."

"Well your name *is* 'Rob'," Marie said.

"We need," Gina said to Angelo, in order to change the subject from Heather's flight and betrayal, "to hear about this new client."

It was the perfect thing to divert the Old Man. "A client? A new client who pays?"

"She definitely pays, Papa," Angelo said. "Though it already seems a long time since I talked to her."

"Lay it out for us, bro," Salvatore said quietly.

Angelo put his wine down and turned so he could see everyone at once. "It begins with a burglary at Crazy Coffee."

"The coffee shop?" Salvatore asked.

"On Saracen Street." Angelo nodded. "Last Friday night a burglar, or burglars, went in through the roof. Has anyone noticed the roofs there?"

No one had.

"Me neither," Angelo said. "But the building Crazy Coffee's in has a flat roof that's above a storeroom and the burglar, or burglars, got in by cutting a hole through it. However, the hole was cut in such a specific and characteristic way that the police immediately thought of our client's husband, Des."

"This Des makes specific holes?" the Old Man said.

"Des is a career burglar for whom this kind of hole is now a trademark."

"Is the hole his whole MO?" Salvatore said.

"We work for a burglar now?" Mama said.

"He pays?" the Old Man said.

"His wife pays," Angelo said. "And we work for her, not him. Her name is Veronica Wigmore."

"What did Des the Drill have to say for himself when the police talked to him?" Salvatore asked.

"Des said nothing." Angelo looked to the others inviting speculation but didn't wait for long. "Because Des is *already* in jail. His wife has not hired us to prove his innocence. When the police realized Des was already locked up, they knew they had to look for someone else."

"Des's in jail but his MO isn't. Interesting." Salvatore stroked his chin.

"In this jail," the Old Man said, "he could teach his holes to a cellmate who gets specific when he gets released."

"True," Angelo said.

"So what *does* the wife want us to do?" Gina said.

Angelo spread his hands, palm up, to invite speculation.

"Does she have some interest in Crazy Coffee?"

"None." After another moment Angelo said, "But Mrs. Wigmore does have an interest in her son."

"A son . . ." the Old Man said. He looked from one to the other of his boys and smiled. "Sons are fine things."

"I'm glad you think so, Papa," Angelo said. "In fact, we've already done work for Mrs. Wigmore's son. On his behalf, anyway."

"Keith Wigmore," Gina said. "A divorce from Kitten Wigmore. Keith had a business and Kitten did the books, until he discovered she was thieving from him. Does anyone remember what kind of business it was?" Now it was Gina's turn to look around the others. When nothing was volunteered she answered her own question. "It was a roofing business."

"Roofs run in the family," Salvatore said.

"Such a memory this girl has," the Old Man said. "You've got a treasure there, Angelo."

Angelo and Gina had reviewed the Wigmore file before he went out. Even so Angelo said, "I know that, Papa. I give thanks for her every day."

"Thanks would be nice even one day," Mama said.

"I'm glad you think that it can be good to have daughters too, Papa," Gina said.

"Speaking of treasures . . ." The Old Man looked around. "So where is Marie? She runs in to give David something and then she runs out again." He looked at his watch. "She doesn't eat?"

"I *would* like to know when she's coming in," Gina said. "It is a school night. Or . . ." Looking at Angelo. "Or do you know what's up with Marie too?"

When Marie's phone rang she nearly jumped out of her seat.

"I know about vibrate mode," Rob said with his crooked smile, "but is yours on electric shock?"

"It's the new ringtone." She fished for the mobile in her bag. "I'm not used to it." She took a deep breath and put on a stern expression as she answered the call without glancing at the screen. She knew full well it would be Jason. "Marie Lunghi here. Who's calling, please?"

"Who's calling is your Uncle Salvatore."

"Oh!" Marie, surprised, softened and then tried to gather herself. "Well, er, how are you?" She was aware that Rob was listening to her, though he'd turned his face away as a politeness.

"I am in exquisite health and sitting in the middle of your living room with your parents and your grandparents, all of whom are wondering about your whereabouts and plans."

"Oh. Well, how nice for you all."

"That's a bit frosty, Marie. I'm beginning to think that you are not alone."

"That's correct."

"Now why would you not want to be your warm, effusive self just because someone is there? Would the person in your company be a male person?"

"It would."

"And what is that noise I hear in the background? Do I recognize the dulcet tones of a public house?"

Marie chuckled in spite of herself. "You're not wrong there."

"Not imbibing alcohol, I trust."

"Heaven forfend."

"Well, your parents, grandparents and I were sitting here discussing the case of the missing Marie. It's quite a mystery. She's been gone all day but then she runs in, and then runs out again followed by her brother. *He* comes back in, but is not himself. But she vanishes."

"Hardly that."

"Without even eating despite a spread of gorgeous and delicious edibles."

"I don't have to come back to eat."

"True. But you do have to come home in order to get a full night's sleep because, I am reliably assured, it's a school night."

"I'm aware of that."

"And you will be back?"

"Of course."

"Soon?"

Marie glanced at the back of Rob's head. "Pretty much."

"I'll reassure your parents and grandparents."

"Thank you."

"Now, the male you're in company with can hear your end of the conversation, right?"

"Well, yes, as a matter of fact."

"Well, just call me Sally when we hang up. He'll be relieved that you aren't talking to another man and that he doesn't have to ask you in order to find that out."

"OK." Marie brightened. She'd been finding it hard to listen and talk and keep track of what Rob must be thinking all at the same time. "Thanks, Sally. Say hello to everyone."

"And get yourself home before it gets late, capiche?"

"That won't be hard either."

"Tatty bye."

"Bye." Marie finished the call, put the mobile away and shrugged to Rob. "Sorry about that."

Rob said, "I hope you weren't put off by my being here."

"Not at all."

"Because I couldn't help hearing you mention food to Sally. I'm just about to order food for myself and I'd love to get something for you too."

"Everyone has those little mobiles nowadays," Mama said with a sigh.

"They've transformed society, Ma," Salvatore said. "You'll be using yours to shop on-line and send emails to Italy before you know it."

"Technology you should keep up," the Old Man said. "Otherwise it passes you by."

"When it's turned on," Gina said.

Salvatore said, "So that's Marie. She'll be home before long and she is fully aware it's a school night. Anyone else you want me to ring? Rosetta? To see if they've locked her up for murder yet?"

"How much longer before your D.I. sees us?" Laurence East asked Officer McCough.

"He'll get here when he gets here, Laurence," Rosetta said.

"But you haven't even eaten yet."

"I'm hardly going to waste away."

"I could get you some coffee," McCough said. "And some biscuits? I, er, I'm not sure what else there is in the machine. I think some crisps and chocolate."

"No thanks."

"I only get the biscuits myself."

"You should have *something*," Laurence said.

"I'd rather wait and have something good at home."

"It *was* delicious there."

"It's not like I've eaten either," McCough said.

"So go find this D.I. of yours and tell him again that we're waiting here, to help *him*."

"I . . . I'm sure he remembers."

Laurence rose. "OK. I'll go."

"Er, please don't."

"Oh, sit down both of you," Rosetta said.

But it was at that moment that the interview room door opened. A bulky man in a dark blue sweater came in. He had an air of authority. "Who've we got here, Felix?"

"Rosetta Lunghi and Laurence East, sir."

"Sit down, Mr. East," the man said.

The big man sat.

"I'm D.I. Phillips. What can I do for you?"

"Our understanding was that it was the other way around," Laurence said.

"They have evidence, sir," McCough said.

"Evidence of what?"

"Well, pertaining to the murder investigation."

Phillips moved toward where Rosetta sat. He seemed to loom over her like the shadow side of a skyscraper. "Not a confession, I take it."

"I took two photographs this afternoon that may include images of the dead man," Rosetta said.

"Really?" Phillips showed measured interest.

"And Laurence thinks he may have seen the same man in the club where he's in charge of security."

"That's Buick's on Walcot Street," Laurence said.

"So they can probably help with identification," McCough said.

"We've already identified the dead man," Phillips said.

"You have? Why wasn't I told?"

"Did you ask, Felix?" Obviously he hadn't. "There was a wallet in his pocket. It contained a driver's licence with a photograph. He also had things with him that enabled us to identify his ex-wife and she's already made a formal identification."

"Oh," McCough said.

"So you won't need us after all?" Rosetta rose and stepped away from the D.I. In fact, Phillips wasn't much taller than she was, though he had twice the bulk.

"I'm still interested in these photographs you say you took of him. Did you know Henry Daniels?"

"I don't know anybody by that name."

"So why the pictures?"

"I'm not even *certain* they are him." She handed the two prints to the detective. "But earlier this afternoon I took some photographs in the area where Cobham Court intersects Walcot Street. They were for a different purpose entirely. But when I checked them I saw a man in the background who was wearing the same colour of jacket as the dead man. I cropped them and enlarged what I had of him."

"It's Daniels, all right. Well well," Phillips said. "When did you take these?"

"Four. Perhaps a little before."

"He was there that early? You're sure of the time?"

"Yes."

"And what was he doing?"

"I have no idea. Laurence and I are members of the Nation Day organizing committee and we were called out because of a dispute at the barrier on Cobham Court. The pictures I took related to that and this man had nothing to do with it. However, he happened to be there."

"Hardly 'happened' but OK . . ." Phillips turned to Laurence. "So did you see Daniels?"

"I didn't notice him at the time. But when I saw the pictures you're holding, he looked familiar. It's that mullah-beard, really. I'm pretty sure I've seen him recently at my club."

"Causing trouble of any kind?"

"No. But we pay attention to the men who are older than most of our usual clientele, especially if they come to the club alone."

"They cause trouble?"

"It's young men getting drunk who are most disruptive, but we've been responding to a police initiative about men spiking women's drinks."

"There's a lot of it about," Phillips said.

"And you think any man who's older who goes to a club alone might be doing *that?*" McCough said.

"We pay attention to anybody who strikes us as different. So, if he's older, and alone . . . That's twice different from our usual crowd."

Phillips said, "Well, the man in these photographs does appear to be Henry Daniels. So tell me, Mr. East, *do* you think Daniels spiked drinks?"

"We never saw it. If we had I'd know the face for sure."

Phillips turned back to Rosetta. "These pictures you took of Daniels, did he know you were taking them?"

"*I* didn't know I was taking pictures of him until I looked at the backgrounds and I have no memory of seeing him there at all. So I've got no idea whether he knew or not."

"He wouldn't have liked it." Phillips raised his eyebrows as he fixed Rosetta's gaze.

"No?"

"Because they prove he was violating a restraining order."

Laurence was the one to react. "Does that mean he was violent?"

"It means," Phillips said, "that he was not allowed within a hundred yards of number three, Cobham Court, or anywhere within a hundred yards of his ex-wife."

"Number three?" Laurence said.

"Yes."

"The ex-wife's name isn't Azaria by any chance, is it?"

"Put your telephone away, Salvatore. Another day you can teach your old-fashioned mother to be part of this century," the Old Man said. "We have Angelo's case to plan, now that we know our Marie will come home for her school night."

Salvatore closed his phone and turned to his brother. "So have I got this right? Mama Bear Wigmore is worried that Papa Bear Wigmore taught Baby Bear Wigmore to cut holes in roofs for purposes of burglary?"

"Yes," Angelo said, "and she wants us to find out if that is what happened."

"Why is this a *detective* case?" Mama asked. "In this modern century with telephones so small you can lose them the mother can talk to the son any old time."

"Mrs. Wigmore would happily ask Keith. However, Baby Bear doesn't talk to his mother."

"He doesn't talk to his *mother?*" Mama said. "What kind of a boy is this?" She glared at each of her sons.

"An angry one who is in therapy," Angelo said.

"Where is Therapy?" the Old Man asked. "It's so far away?"

"He should get a refund, this sick boy," Mama said. "A

therapy should *fix* him."

"Ah, therapy-treatment," the Old Man said. "Again I am stupid. Huh!" He sipped from his wine.

Angelo said, "I think it worked the other way, Mama. Because of the therapy he decided that his mother and Kitten, his ex-wife, are like each other—controlling, devious and manipulative."

Mama was all but out of her chair with indignation. "He calls his *mother* such names?"

"He sent her a letter."

"For this she gave birth to him? Made his meals? Ironed his shirts?"

"The son blames his mother for his wife?" the Old Man asked.

"I could give such a boy some therapy," Mama said, crossing her arms tightly across her chest.

"Would you like to be the one who talks to him, Mama?" Angelo asked.

Mama blinked for a moment, digesting what she had been asked. It had been a long time since she last participated actively in a case. But this situation was special. "Yes," she said. "Sign me up."

"So Sally is a flatmate of yours?" Rob asked.

"In the sense that Sally has a room in the flat," Marie said, which was true.

"That does rather sound like the definition."

"Even if Sally hardly ever sleeps there?" Which was also true. Her uncle's old room still had a bed but was used mostly for storage.

"Sounds ideal." Rob held up his hands. "Not that I'm saying anything against Sally, but someone who shares the rent but doesn't take up space . . . Where can I get myself one of those?"

"It would certainly feel more crowded at home if Sally was

around all the time."

"Are there a lot of you?"

"Six, counting Sally, but it's a big place."

"It must be. But you have a room of your own?"

"Of course."

"Though I expect you're in and out of each other's rooms all the time anyway."

"Hardly," Marie said. "Why would I want them in my room or to go into their poxy rooms?"

"I just thought if there are a lot of you, you'd be partying non-stop. Students and all that."

"Only one of the others is a student, and a geek with no chic at that. And I can't even remember the last time there was a party there." Did birthday dinners around the big table count? But that would not be the "partying" Rob meant—people drinking and dancing and chatting each other up and looking for places to snog. Some chance of *that* at home.

"Early to bed because they have to be early to rise for jobs?"

"It's *very* boring. Socially, I mean."

"But you must like it for some reason," Rob said. "Otherwise a live-wire like you would be looking for somewhere else."

Marie contemplated for a moment whether she actually liked living at home. There were definite advantages, but it would be far *cooler* to have her own place. One where no Uncle Sallys called her to check on where she was and when she was coming home. If she was sharing with Cassie, for instance, they *could* have parties, and boys around, and drink or smoke if they damn well pleased. "I would *love* to be somewhere livelier, and with friends. But, you're right, it is very convenient."

"And cheap?"

"That too," Marie said.

"But maybe if you get this business of yours off the ground . . ." Rob said.

At which point their food arrived.

Phillips stared coldly at Laurence. "Do you know Azaria Daniels, Mr. East?"

"Only because we met her today." Laurence turned to Rosetta, seeming suddenly unsettled.

"*She's* the dead man's ex-wife?" Rosetta said. How extreme did a man's behaviour have to be to warrant a restraining order? Did it mean he was, like, *stalking* her?

"So you both know Azaria Daniels?" Phillips looked from one to the other of them, one eyebrow raised.

"She was one of the Cobham Court residents supervising the barrier today. We met her at the incident that led to my taking the photographs," Rosetta said.

"Are any of your photographs of Mrs. Daniels?"

"No. She was behind me as I was taking them."

"Behind you?"

"Yes."

"So she was looking the same way you were?"

"I can only assume she was looking in that general direction. The girls causing the trouble were very loud and very aggressive."

"So you assume she was looking in the general direction of her ex-husband?"

Rosetta shrugged. "My attention was on the girls causing the trouble, and those who seemed to be with them. The pictures I got of Mr. Daniels show him closer to the corner."

Phillips turned to Laurence. "Did you see where Mrs. Daniels was looking?"

Laurence shook his head vigorously. "I was at the barrier with those awful girls shouting at me."

"So when did you meet Mrs. Daniels?"

"After the incident was over Rosetta and I went to The Bell

for a drink with her."

"So you went for a *drink* with Mrs. Daniels." Phillips made it sound as if they'd been holding this information back.

Which slightly annoyed Rosetta. "A drink, *and* cashew nuts. Both salted and dry-roasted."

"Did Mrs. Daniels speak of her ex-husband over your drinks and cashew nuts?"

"I don't remember her saying anything about an ex-husband. Do you, Laurence?"

He shook his head as he said, "We talked mostly about the crazy guy across the road who throws things out his windows."

"Ah, the legendary Nazi," Phillips said.

"You know about him, then?"

"We all know about *him.*"

"I don't," Felix McCough said.

Rosetta had all but forgotten McCough was in the room but a look from Phillips kept McCough from asking to be filled in. Phillips said, "And was this drink in The Bell the last time either of you talked with Mrs. Daniels?"

"She was standing outside her building when Laurence and I went to Cobham Court the second time," Rosetta said. "I didn't speak to her but Laurence and she stood next to one another."

"We did?"

Addressing Phillips, Rosetta said, "Laurence and I were helping to count the Nation Day collection money when our Chair, Barbara Morris, came in to tell us about the dead man. We all went out to see what had happened. When I saw where the body was lying, it crossed my mind that my pictures might conceivably be useful. So I left Laurence to find a police officer." She nodded to McCough. "I explained the situation to Officer McCough and he went to speak to you. While I was waiting for him to come back, I remember noticing that Laurence was standing with Azaria."

Phillips turned back to Laurence, who said, "Oh yes. I remember now."

"And the nature of *this* conversation with Mrs. Daniels?"

Laurence shrugged. "I suppose it was along the lines of 'We meet again,' and 'Do you know what's happening?' "

"And did she know what was happening?"

"She said she'd heard more clamour—that was her word, now that I think about it. She looked out her window, saw all the police and came down to see what was going on."

"That's all she said?"

Laurence tried to remember. "That's all," he said. "We were only there for a few minutes and then that guy stole Rosetta's mobile."

Back to Rosetta. "Your mobile was stolen?"

"I took the card out with the pictures in case you—one of you—wanted to look at them. So I was holding it and then what happened was—"

Phillips held up a hand. "I don't think I'm all that interested in the details of the theft, Ms. Lunghi, unless you think it might relate to the death of Mr. Daniels."

"I don't see how it could. It struck me as an opportunist theft."

"Nothing to do with Mrs. Daniels either, then?"

Rosetta shook her head.

Phillips turned to Laurence. "Think again about your last conversation with Mrs. Daniels."

Laurence's brow furrowed. "All right."

"Was there anything in Mrs. Daniels's demeanour, or tone of voice, that suggested she was uncomfortable, or nervous, or anything other than just a curious bystander?"

"No. Nothing like that."

"So she was chatting away, about nothing in particular, while her ex-husband's body was lying across the street and the police were investigating his violent death?"

Laurence had nothing to say to that. Rosetta said, "To be fair, the body was covered by then."

To Laurence Phillips said, "After the theft of the phone, what did you talk about with Mrs. Daniels?"

"Nothing. Rosetta ran after the thief. I followed after her."

"Has either of you talked with Mrs. Daniels again?"

"No." Both.

Phillips addressed McCough. "We have Ms. Lunghi's and Mr. East's contact details, I take it, Felix?"

"Yes, sir."

"Show them out, then, will you?" To Rosetta and Laurence, "Thank you for your patience. We may need to be in touch again."

"OK, tell me if *I'm* stupid again," the Old Man said, "but this mixed-up boy, Keith, who rejects his mother, how stupid is *he?*"

"What are you thinking, Papa?" Angelo said.

"His father is in jail."

"Yes."

"From cutting holes that the police recognize."

"Yes."

Salvatore whispered to Gina, "A hole was cut in the Crazy Coffee roof last night. Police are looking into it."

"Hush," Gina mouthed.

The Old Man said, "So why would a boy with any brain copy such a father's MO? These holes put the father in jail. These are the holes *not* to cut, aren't they?"

"That's a good point," Angelo said.

"Sounds like you should go visit the father, Papa," Gina said.

"Visit this father who is in jail?" the Old Man said. "*I* should?"

Angelo sat up. "I assumed I'd go to Langnorton, given that I'm the one who's talked with Mrs. Wigmore."

"Does that matter," Gina asked, "if all we're trying to find out is who he taught this technique to?"

"But it's out of town."

"I'm not just stupid now?" the Old Man said. "Now I also can't drive?"

"I never said that, Papa," Angelo said.

"I agree with your wife. It was my idea, to cut holes is bad. I should go."

The younger Lunghis looked from one to the other.

"Good," Mama said. "We will bust this case together, you and me, old man." She took her husband's hand. She smiled when he squeezed hers back.

Once Rosetta and Laurence got to the bottom of the steps in front of the police station, they paused. Rosetta was beginning to feel hungry and certainly intended to head for home. Given that Laurence had already eaten, there was no real reason for them to walk together unless it turned out he lived in the direction of Walcot Street. But it was rude just to set off even though she found herself less interested in being around him than she had been earlier in the day.

However, whether they would go their separate ways was not uppermost in Laurence's mind because he said, "Do you think that D.I. Phillips *really* believes Azaria is involved in her husband's death?"

"It sounded that way."

Laurence's face wrinkled up. "It just seems so . . . so unlikely."

"It *is* odd if Azaria really didn't notice her ex-husband in Cobham Court. It's not like the area between Walcot Street and the barrier was big, and you do tend to recognize people you know, even in crowds." Especially, she thought, people you've taken out restraining orders against.

"I suppose."

"Her not having recognized his body lying across the street is more understandable, even if she did see it before he was covered up. It's quite possible she didn't know the jacket or see the face."

"The police were keeping spectators away," Laurence said.

"Was she already standing outside when we got there?"

Laurence considered. "You ducked under the tape to talk to the police. That's when I noticed she was standing outside her building."

"So we don't know when she came down."

"No." He shook his head. "But do you really think she's the type to be *involved* in, you know, a *death?*"

"What type does it take, Laurence?"

He shrugged his massive shoulders. "Your family's in the crime-busting business."

"Hardly. Most of our work is for solicitors and insurance companies and the 'crimes' we work on tend to be a matter of which side you've been hired by."

"I've been trying to remember what Azaria and I talked about the second time. But I'm sure it was nothing . . . you know . . . significant."

"Did you feel she was nervous? Or anxious? Did she keep trying to look past you rather than at you as you talked? Did she seem preoccupied?"

"I didn't notice anything like that, but we were both interested in what the police were doing. I don't think we said much at all, to tell the truth."

They stood in silence for a moment, thinking about the scene at Cobham Court. But their ruminations were interrupted as the door they'd come out of was opened again. A woman said emphatically, "I'll be *fine*. Just leave me *alone*."

Rosetta and Laurence turned to the voice to discover that the speaker was none other than the beautiful woman from number three, Cobham Court, herself. Her eyes were closed as she stood at the top of the short flight of steps. She exhaled with relief as the door closed behind her.

"Azaria?" Laurence said.

The eyes popped wide open. Rosetta had a momentary sense that there was fear in Azaria's face after the surprise of hearing her name. Fear, or guilt.

But then it was gone. Azaria recognized Rosetta and Laurence. "Little and Large?" she said. "What are you two doing here?"

"As a matter of fact," Rosetta said, "we've just been talking with the police about you."

"About *me?*" Azaria hesitated at the top of the steps. Was she reluctant to join them? Her only option, however, was to go back into the police station, so she finally descended the steps, saying, "*What* about me?"

"A D.I. Phillips took us through everything we'd seen and heard at the crime scene," Laurence said, "as well as the conversations we'd all had."

"I suppose they must be interviewing everyone. I've just finished giving my statement to a D.C. Young, I think her name was. She wanted me to wait for one of their lot to drive me home but I'm perfectly capable of walking a mile."

"It probably wasn't an issue of your capability," Rosetta said. "She may just have felt you might be upset."

"Ah," Azaria said. "So you know it was Henry who died."

"It must have been a shock. No matter what your current relationship with him was."

After a moment Azaria said, "Yes. Of course you're right." She frowned. "How much of *my* history did your D.I. Whatsisface see fit to tell you?"

"Only that the dead man was your ex-husband and that there was a restraining order on him," Rosetta said.

"So you won't think me utterly unfeeling if I say that it was almost as big a shock to know that the bastard was outside my house again."

"It sounds *very* disturbing," Laurence said. "All of it."

"You're not wrong there," Azaria said.

"So you didn't know he was in the neighbourhood?" Rosetta said.

"I most certainly did not."

"Because Laurence thinks he may have seen him in a local club earlier in the week."

"Bloody hell," Azaria said.

"So when did you first know he was in Bath?" Rosetta asked.

"*Know* that Henry had found me? When I saw him on the slab in the RUH mortuary. Though they did tell me beforehand it was probably him."

"Oh dear," Laurence said. "Going from the RUH to the police station . . ." He shook his head sympathetically.

"I didn't want it all hanging over me. Better to get it all down and done in one nasty gulp."

"So you didn't see your ex-husband when he was outside your place earlier?"

Azaria jerked as if she'd been poked. "He was out there earlier *today?*"

"He was hanging around during the trouble at the barrier."

Azaria studied Rosetta in the fading light. "How the hell do you know that? Did you know Henry or something?"

"It turns out he was in the background of a couple of the pictures I took of those awful girls."

"Was he, by God." Azaria's hand went to her mouth and she shook her head behind it. "He was *in* your pictures? He wouldn't have liked that."

"So the policeman said."

"You had your mobile stolen though. Did you get it back?"

Rosetta shook her head. "But I'd taken out the card with the pictures on it."

"I can't pretend to understand what that means," Azaria said. "But if Henry knew you had pictures of him outside my building, I'd have put money on his being the one who stole your phone. Except that by then he was already dead."

"What a horrible day for you," Laurence said. He touched her supportively on the arm. "Look, we're going your way. Let us walk you back to your building."

"To make sure I don't collapse in tears in the middle of Bog Island?" But before either Laurence or Rosetta could respond to that, Azaria said, "Yes, thanks. If you're already going that way, I'd appreciate a little moral support. That's nice of you."

"That was really nice of you," Marie said after finishing a baguette and taking some of Rob's chips. "Thank you."

"Got to make sure our poor, beleaguered students keep strong," Rob said. "Fancy a drink to wash it down? I'm having one." He rose. "Or coffee? What would you like?"

Marie didn't want to be a wuss. "A vodka and orange, please, before I head home. But let me pay for these." She hunted in her bag for her purse.

"No, please," Rob said. "I wouldn't think of it."

"I'm not *that* beleaguered. And if you don't mind getting them for us, then I can pack my things up." Not that Marie had much to gather, but she certainly didn't want to give the barman a chance to ask her for ID. "Plus, you're closer."

"A girl who pays her own way. Be still my heart." Rob took the note Marie handed him.

While she watched him go to the bar she wondered whether a fiver was going to be enough. Not that she had any more to offer. Apart from the change at the bottom of her bag. There was always at least a *little* down there. But after a moment she decided not to look. The fiver had shown willing. If Rob wanted an expensive drink he could make up the difference.

It's a funny old life, she thought. She'd come into the pub because she was furious with Jason and she wanted to send him a really stinging text message, but now she hadn't given the unreliable idiot so much as a single thought for ages. She was still curious what he thought he was up to, leaving her so abruptly, especially after the unprecedented affection they'd shared during the day. But it didn't matter to her now, at least not in the way it had when she arrived.

Marie figured that she probably wasn't going to end up being all that interested in Jason anyway. He was confident and forceful, and older—which did carry some prestige at school. But being older, he carried baggage with him. His obsession with business, for instance. And his odd neighbour girl, Jennifer—there was something odd about the way she thought she had a role in Jason's life, though he denied it. Besides, Rob was far older than Jason. And if he wasn't forceful in the way Jason was, he was still confident and the way he expressed it included paying more attention to *her* than Jason ever did. Jason may have talked to her, but he was probably even thinking about networking when they were kissing.

The thought of Jason's brain whirling away during a prolonged kiss quite amused Marie. The truth was that during most of their kisses Marie's mind had been whirling away too, working out how she was going to describe them to Cassie.

Rob returned with the drinks. "Vodka and orange for the hardworking student who is letting her hair down an inch or two on this Sunday evening." He put the glass and orange bottle in front of Marie. "And a half of best for myself. Thank you." Once he was settled in his own seat he pushed some coins across the table. "Your change."

"Thanks," Marie said. She mixed about half the orange in

with the vodka and lifted her glass. "Cheers."

"Cheers."

Marie tasted the sharpness of the vodka but was pleased that she hadn't dumped the whole bottle of orange in this time.

7

As Rosetta, Laurence and Azaria approached the wide place in Walcot Street where the main stage had stood earlier in the day, Rosetta got a sudden flashback image of all the food that had been laid out on the kitchen table at home. There must be plenty left. She asked Azaria, "Have you eaten?"

"Well, no."

"Because my family's house is just ahead here, and we have plenty of food already prepared. Laurence can attest to its quality."

Responding to Azaria's glance, Laurence said, "On the way to the police station one of the cops wanted to look at the pictures Rosetta took. While I was waiting her mother filled a plate for me—they're very hospitable. And it *was* good. Delicious, in fact."

"It's a kind thought," Azaria said, "but I'd really prefer to go home now. I'm not feeling hungry but if I find my appetite later, I've got things in that I can make."

They arrived at the Lunghis' door. Laurence said, "*You* haven't eaten either, Rosetta. Why don't you go on up. I'll walk with Azaria."

It seemed that Laurence was hoping for a chance to be alone with the beautiful Azaria. But she might have murdered one man today already. Rosetta would have felt *so* guilty if anything bad were to happen to Laurence . . . "I'll come along," she said.

"I wouldn't mind another look at where it all happened."

David was tired from his emotionally exhausting day, but he was far too buzzy even to *think* about bed or sleep. "*Thank you* for emailing me," Lara had written back to him. "I'm doing things for Mum now, but I'll write again later if she manages to fall asleep."

Lara's dealings with her mother were puzzling, even mysterious. But it was the italics in the "*Thank you*" that particularly excited David. The message was brief, but he read it over and over again.

Between times it crossed his mind to use the evening to get on with some of his projects. But he found it hard to concentrate. Hard? It was bloody impossible. Was this what love was?

He lay on his bed, breathing quickly. Visualizing Lara . . .

Yet how *stupid* was it to be thinking of love—*love?*—with respect to someone he'd never had a private conversation with, never been alone with, never kissed?

The thought of kissing Lara definitely gave David italics. He lingered on the notion of it, the image of it. He tilted his head to the right, as he would do in a real kiss in order to avoid a clash of noses. He puckered up.

Then he shook himself and shifted to a sitting position. Marie was right. For someone so clever he could be really stupid sometimes.

And yet there were the italics in "*Thank you*" . . .

Mmmmm.

There was a knock on David's door. The unexpected sound made him jump off the bed, his spine tingling, fizzing. "What!" It was a shout. He hadn't intended that.

"I just wanted to be sure you're all right." It was his father.

"I'm fine." He said that louder than intended too. Should he say sorry?

"Nothing you want? Nothing I can get you? Something else to eat? Or maybe we can talk a bit?"

"I'm fine, Dad. Really." Better. Calmer.

"Really?"

"Really."

"Well, OK then."

David sensed that his father was still there, waiting on the other side of the door. He wondered if there was something he could say, maybe to thank his dad for the trip to the pub earlier.

But then David's computer made the noise that meant things were happening. David rushed to the screen. A moment later the machine's voice said, "You've got mail."

"Well," the Old Man said as he shifted forward on the couch, readying himself to get to his feet, "big day tomorrow, seeing about going to jail, unless there's more business."

"Nothing else, Papa," Gina said. Then Angelo returned to the room. "Is there any more business to deal with tonight?"

"Don't think so. Unless you have something for us, Sally." He glanced at his brother.

"Me?" Salvatore said. "When was the last time *I* brought a case in?"

"Nothing more then." Angelo dropped back into the settee beside his wife and picked up his wine glass. "David says he's fine."

"*Says?* You didn't see him?" Gina said.

"We talked through the door. But he's fine."

"So he's fine," the Old Man said. He rose. "Mama, you come?"

Mama rose too. "I'll just check the kitchen."

Gina said, "Everything's done, Mama."

"You didn't get David's plate?" Mama said to Angelo.

"It'll keep, Mama," Angelo said. "Sleep well."

Mama nodded and headed with her husband for the landing and the stairs up to their flat. It took them through the kitchen. Mama hesitated by the sink.

"What? David's plate?" The Old Man headed for the stairs.

Mama followed. Her tomorrow was a big day too. She had a son to talk to. One who was maybe stupid enough to drill holes. One who was certainly stupid, if he wouldn't speak to his mother.

The Old Man opened the door to their flat and waited for her outside it.

"What?" she said when she arrived.

"I can't open a door?"

She said nothing. Then, as she passed by him to go in, the Old Man took her by the waist and pulled her close with a hug. Then he kissed her lips.

Mama was startled but kissed back.

"You see what happens?" he said.

"What happens?"

"They give me a job to do with this father in prison and his holes. Something that isn't a mobile call or sticking stamps. It's because I exercise in the gym. And I go to the gym because you got it in your head. So thank you."

"You're *thank-youing* me?"

"Where it's deserved."

Mama smiled. "Thank you for thank-youing."

He opened the door. "You too have a job."

"I *always* have jobs." She went in. "I don't need gym exercise for jobs."

"To nag some mother's son? For this you've been exercising all your life."

As they turned the corner into Cobham Court, Rosetta saw that the police tape was still in place. A uniformed officer,

132

posted to guard the area, looked bored.

Azaria led the trio across the street before turning toward her building. It kept them away from the taped-off area. Hardly surprising, Rosetta thought. No matter what her recent relations with the dead man—even if all she felt at Henry Daniels's death was pure relief—the events of the day *must* have disturbed her.

Outside number three, Azaria faced her companions. "You really didn't have to walk me all the way back, but thank you. It's very kind of you both."

"No problem," Laurence said quickly, heartily.

"Glad to," Rosetta said.

"I'm *dying* for a cup of tea, if that isn't a terribly insensitive word to use in the circumstances," Azaria said. "Will you come up? Have one too?"

Rosetta took this invitation to be one of politeness but Laurence said, "If you're sure you're up to it, I'd love one."

Azaria turned to the door with her key. "Of course."

It seemed to be expected that Rosetta would come up too. So she did, following the other two up one flight of stairs to a small landing.

Rosetta genuinely fancied a cup of tea. It would have been easy enough to go home and get one—and lovely food with it—but she was happy to go to Azaria's. The immediate appeal of a look at the flat was quite specific: to see just what parts of Cobham Court could be seen from Azaria's windows.

"Mum's asleep now," Lara wrote, "though she's on the couch and I'll have to move her later. Maybe you're asleep too, David? But if so then maybe you get up early and check your email? So you could still see this before you get to school? I hope so, because then you'll know how glad I am that you're not really really pissed off with me. It might probably be hard to tell you that at school with all those other people around. I wouldn't blame you for being pissed off, I really wouldn't. But I'm *glad* you're not."

The italics again . . . David, too, was *glad.*

"And it's not just because you're my only friend so far in Bath," Lara continued. "It's because you're so nice. I *wanted* to tell you that this afternoon. You showed me around and weren't impatient or showy-offy, even though you've got plenty to show off about plus your interesting family. Oh, I've heard all about you, David Lunghi, yes I have. In PE some girls tried to tease me for how Miss Hamlish put us together and how I probably didn't understand a word you said because you're so clever. But I like how you talk and as soon as I said that they sang a different tune. They told me about how all the teachers think you're great, and how you have detectives for a family, and how Marie is great in drama, but mostly about how they admire you. You have fans in this school, yes you do, and I wouldn't blame you for spending your time with them instead of someone who let you down like I did today, even though it wasn't because I wanted to."

There was a space in the email then. Lara explained it as she began her next line. "I've been sitting at the screen here for ages—probably while you're dreaming away about clever things. It's just that I know things about your family, which is all great, and I hope you'll tell me more one day too. But there is something you ought to know about my family and it's not good, even though it's why we moved to Bath like we did and it's also why I let you down today. Well, sort of. And I really ought to tell you because, well, for example, when Marie's boyfriend, Jason, saw me home after she went upstairs with my letter to you, he just assumed you and I are boyfriend and girlfriend too, and he might probably tell other people that's what we are too. OK, I could have set him straight but he was talking away about other things like his plans and how great it is that you and I know stuff about programming computers and that he doesn't. But I really don't want to reflect badly on you or your family at school. I don't want to be forward, or to assume things, but your email was, well, friendly like that and I *would* like to get to know you better if you'd like to get to know me. It's just that there's this thing."

The "thing" could have been from outer space as far as David was concerned, once he read—and reread, and read again—"I *would* like to get to know you better if you'd like to get to know me."

Yes! Yes! He got up and danced around the room. He was bursting with the excitement of it. He would even have told Marie if she'd been there to tell. Lara *liked* him. Own italics supplied.

"My round," Rob said. He stood. "Yours is a vodka, but would you like another orange with it or do you have enough left in the bottle?"

Marie looked at her bottle, which *was* about half full. As opposed to half empty. She sucked her lips to keep from giggling, although this vodka and orange wasn't having nearly the effect on her that the first one in the Chameleon had in the afternoon. Maybe it was because she'd just eaten. Maybe that thing about not drinking on an empty stomach wasn't just an old wives' tale. Or *maybe* she was just becoming an experienced drinker really fast. Maybe it was one of her many natural talents. "Just another vodka," she said. A bit of a giggle slipped out.

Azaria's flat occupied the second and third floors of number three and was accessed from the first floor by a flight of green-carpeted stairs. The walls on the way up were hung with framed film and music posters and as Rosetta reached the top she came face-to-face with a poster that combined the two. It was for a film titled *Performance* and the two pictures on it were both of Mick Jagger. However, the two images were very different from each other. Was the poster there because it had a message about the multiple roles any one person plays in the world? Did Azaria think of life as a performance?

Rosetta's hostess passed the poster without comment and led her visitors to the living room. "I'm having tea," she said, "but if either of you would prefer coffee, or perhaps something stronger, just say. Anything's possible."

"I'd love some tea," Rosetta said.

"Yes, tea, please," Laurence said. He seemed to fill the room by himself, although it was not small.

"Tea bags all right?"

"Of course," Rosetta said.

"And how do you each take it?"

"Just milk for me."

"Milk and two sugars, please," Laurence said. "What a great place you have here."

"Thank you," Azaria said. " "I'll be in the kitchen but do make yourselves comfortable." She left.

Places to sit in the room were provided by two colourful couches placed at right angles to each other. A small upholstered chair was in the corner opposite them. A second low chair was half-hidden at the end of one of the couches and faced a small television. Given that most living rooms these days are organized around the TV, the arrangement was a pretty clear message that any tele-viewing Azaria did, she did alone.

However, Laurence was not interested in sitting or the TV. He moved around the room looking at the pictures on the wall. "It's like an art gallery," he said in a hushed voice.

Rosetta could see what he meant. There were paintings and drawings on all the walls and sculptures and photographs rested on the tops of the bookshelves and above the fireplace. However, what most struck Rosetta at first glance was how clean everything was, and how tidy. Nor had Azaria offered the conventional apology for unexpected guests, about how unprepared everything was. It was as if everything had a place and was damn well in it. It seemed that Azaria's was a very organized mind.

Or had she, perhaps, been expecting guests? Or had visitors already? Either way, or neither, Rosetta was suddenly very conscious of the fact that Azaria did not share her flat with four other people, including two teenagers. And she also probably didn't have her parents living in the same building and visiting daily. Rosetta felt a momentary urge to have a place of her own.

In the Lunghis' household everyone felt free to enter her room with little more than a cursory knock of warning. Imagine, though. A place of her *own*. There was something both calming and exciting about such a prospect.

Ah well. Maybe one day . . .

And then Rosetta realized what had just happened. Her usual daydream about the future was to see herself living somewhere as part of a couple. She couldn't remember ever yearning to be alone before. Had she discovered something new in herself?

Laurence, meanwhile, had completed his examination of the pictures on the wall. "Do you think all these are real?"

"Real" was not what he meant, but Rosetta understood. But although the pictures *were* oils or water colours or charcoals, she was more interested in their subjects. Several were of people, perhaps family? But on one bit of wall a cat at the centre of a swirl of smoke was paired with a dog lying in the dark beneath a full moon. And at opposite ends of the room large pictures of birds faced each other. One, a falcon, surveyed its domain. The other was gulping a fish.

Was Azaria intending something symbolic by having two birds

of prey—one a devourer of red meat, the other of sea creatures—face each other at opposite ends of the room, bounding it? If things didn't happen accidentally in Azaria's world, then perhaps she was. And if the cat and dog were paired, though opposites in species, did that comment on the nature of the relationship between the people whose portraits hung together?

"And so many books," Laurence said. He began a second circuit of the room, examining the bookcases that lined all the available walls, although only up to about waist-height. Waist-height for a normal-sized person.

Rosetta was tiring of his exclamations, so she didn't respond. Instead, she moved to one of the two windows that overlooked Cobham Court.

"And all the CDs . . ."

Standing close to the window, Rosetta could see the roadway below clearly, all the way to the intersection with Walcot Street. Even standing back a little she had a good view of the police tape and the bored officer guarding it.

However, the distance to where the body had been found, as well as the angles involved, made it virtually certain that the dead man's injury had not come from someone in these windows throwing a heavy object onto his head. Not that the police had ever suggested that was what happened to Henry Daniels. Perhaps Rosetta just had things being thrown from windows in her mind because of the Nazi across the street.

She looked across to the Nazi's window. It *was* above where Daniels had been found. The window was open even now, a gap of a couple of feet with the pane supported by a stack of beer cans.

Although . . . Rosetta frowned. Nobody had actually said that Daniels's body was found in the same place he had been attacked. She'd been assuming that whatever happened to the dead man had occurred where he fell. Which need not be the case.

The truth was that Rosetta knew nothing for sure about how Henry Daniels had received his injury. Was it *possible* that he'd been beneath Azaria's window and that something had dropped onto his head? That he had then staggered across the road to end up beneath the Nazi's window?

It could even have been an accident. Azaria might have seen Daniels outside, opened the window to lean out and shout at him, knocked something heavy from the sill that happened to hit her ex on the head.

Rosetta looked at the sill. It was bare—unlike the sill of the other window in the room, the one farther from Walcot Street. She looked more closely. Was that a stain? A mark that something had left? In this extremely tidy flat? It was hard to be sure in the fading light, but it looked like it might be.

Or, it might even not have been an accident. She'd said it was a shock that Daniels had discovered where she lived now. Perhaps when she saw him below she just grabbed whatever was closest at hand to chuck at him, to scare him, to say, "Go away!" She might just have failed to miss her target . . .

Rosetta looked down at the roadway, trying to picture the scenario she was considering. Suppose something like that *had* happened. How could one try to confirm it?

Well, apart from checking the possible stain on the window sill, one could check the pavement below Azaria's window to see if there were bloodstains. Or perhaps a trail of stains that led across the street. Well, "one" couldn't, but the police could. The area in front of number three was outside the police tape. Had they even thought to look more widely?

Would there necessarily *be* stains? Wasn't it true that a first blow to someone's head was often less bloody than any that followed? But in any case, mightn't whatever was dropped—or thrown—still be down there somewhere?

Rosetta looked through the window again. Then, seeing that the top half was already open, she pulled on the bottom sash. It slid up easily. She stretched out to look straight down. Below her, iron railings protected pedestrians from a stairway that led down to the building's basement and vaults. Something hard could easily have bounced off Daniels's head and dropped into the stairwell where it would be unnoticed. It could even be there now.

Unless Azaria had already gone down to fetch it, bring it back up, wash it off, and return it to its *place*. Nevertheless, forensic examination might still produce evidence of what had happened. Blood, or a bit of stone from the pavement, or a bit of black paint from the iron railings or the stairs down to the basement . . .

Rosetta brought herself back into the room. Laurence was standing at the mantelpiece. He put down a woman's head and reached for a metal sculpture of interlinked figures. It was like a metal ball. Perfect for . . . "Don't touch that," Rosetta called.

Laurence jumped back and turned to her.

"It could be . . . valuable."

He looked at the metal figures. "You think?"

"You don't want to take the chance of damaging it, do you?"

"I suppose not. *Quite* a place though, isn't this?"

"Yes," Rosetta said. "Beautiful."

"What do you think she does?" Laurence asked. "For a living, I mean."

"No idea."

"Something arty, I bet." He continued his latest trip around the room. How many had he already made?

Rosetta returned to her aerial view of Cobham Court. Again she stretched out the window, looking down. It was impossible to make out any details in the stairwell. So, *could* there be a murder weapon somewhere down there in the dark? She was shocked to be thinking such things. But it was shocking that a violent death had occurred so close, just a few hours before. And that the dead man was connected to the woman in whose flat she now stood.

A shiver passed down her spine.

But then she shook herself. This was all silliness. There would have been witnesses to anything untoward that happened. If there was one day on which the Walcot Street area was *packed* with potential witnesses it was Nation Day.

And not just on the street. Every balcony or bit of projecting roof seemed to have had at least a few people on it at one time or another. That was the thing about Nation Day. There was a constant stream of costumed people and performing groups joining the milling throngs on the street, all day long. In good weather, like today, sitting out in the sun with friends, watching the events below and sharing a drink and a smoke, was a wonderfully sociable thing to do. So people did it. All along the street.

A flat area on the roof of the Nazi's building could be reached through a dormer window, so even that had probably had people out on it enjoying themselves, although nobody was out there now.

And yet . . . for all the potential witnesses, *so* much was going on that events that might attract attention at some other time could go unnoticed in the melee. Suppose an object *had* come out of this window and hit Henry Daniels on the head and then rolled away. If there was no reason for people to be watching Daniels, or the building, and if all that happened afterwards was that Daniels staggered across the street, then who would notice *that*? Because another thing that Nation Day had plenty of was drunks. By late in the afternoon, there was no shortage of staggering people in the Walcot Nation.

And there must have been a lot of things thrown or dropped into the street during the day from the many informal vantage points. Intentionally or otherwise. Would anyone have noticed that the Nazi was throwing things if he hadn't thrown a bottle that "exploded" as it hit the roadway? Did anyone know even now whether he'd thrown anything else before the bottle?

Rosetta brought herself back into the room.

Behind her Azaria said, "More excitement out there?"

"No no, just looking," Rosetta said. "I wanted to see how they're getting along with cleaning up."

"I forgot that you two have official duties today. Is there some job you're meant to be doing now?"

"No, no," Laurence said. "Our assignment today was security."

And helping to count the money. Rosetta had completely forgotten about that, what with everything else that had happened. "Laurence, do you know if Barbara and Stephanie got people to go back for the count?"

The big man shrugged. "Bound to have."

"What *count?*" Azaria said. She made it sound like she was asking about royalty.

"We were working our way through the money that was taken today when Barbara, our organizing committee's Chair, came in to tell us about . . . well, about what happened. She was very upset about it being during Nation Day."

"I can understand that," Azaria said quietly.

"Laurence and I probably ought to look in at the office after we leave here."

Laurence frowned. "Do you think?"

"Besides, we mustn't stay here long, for Azaria's sake."

When David returned to the computer screen to read "I *would* like to get to know you better if you'd like to get to know me" one more time, he went on to what Lara had written about the family "thing" that she felt was a problem.

"I don't know how to say this to make it nice," she wrote. "My father's in jail. He's already been there for more than four years. Do you know what GBH means? In his case it meant beating someone up when he was drunk, including hitting him with a stone. He missed the man's head but broke his shoulder. So I'm the daughter of a violent felon. Life just hasn't been the same since it all happened."

David paused to consider this. Was this *it?* He couldn't imagine how anything Lara's father had done would interfere with things between Lara and himself. The idea of *things* between them excited David. Something *happening* excited him again. It was a moment or two before he could continue.

"Dad's behaved himself in jail," Lara wrote. "He was always fine if he was sober. It was only when he'd get drunk, then it was like he was a different person. But his good behaviour's got him moved to Langnorton, which is an 'open prison' a bit north of Bath. Have you heard of it? In fact, it's very good for a GBH convict to be allowed there. And he'll maybe even be on a day-release job sometime unless he does something bad. And it's because of all that that Mum and I moved here—to be closer to him and make it easier for Mum to visit. I visit too, even though he doesn't like me to see him in prison, but I don't go so often during term time and especially not now when exams are coming up. He's got a little over a year to go, unless he loses some remission. Mum intended to visit him today—which was when I thought I'd be able to come out to meet you—only there was some problem about not enough guards on duty. When she called they told her not to come. You get in the habit of checking things like that when you visit jails a lot. It's horrible to make the trip and not be allowed in. I don't really understand how it all works there. Maybe with your family's business you understand and you can explain it to me—you explain things so well. Oops. She's awake. Got to go. xxx"

xxx! David was in heaven. He wouldn't have minded if Lara's father was a serial killer. He probably wouldn't even have minded if *she* was.

After Mama and the Old Man went upstairs, Salvatore remained in the living room with Gina and Angelo. "I won't stay long," he said, "but it's comforting to be in the bosom of my family . . ." He poured himself a fresh glass of wine.

"You're always welcome here," Gina said.

"Wouldn't want to keep you guys up, though. Tell me if it gets late for you."

"We won't turn in until Marie gets back."

"Or until we find out about Rosetta," Angelo said.

"If they'd arrested her, I think we'd already know," Salvatore said.

"Ah, but how did she get on with that Laurence."

"The big guy?"

"Mama was very taken with him."

"Mama would greet a wife-murderer being released from prison by saying, 'So, would I be right that you're single now?' "

"*Bad* Salvatore," Gina said.

"You no like-a me to tell old-a jokes?" Salvatore reached for his jacket pocket. "How's about I ring Rose then?"

"No, no."

"It's not a school night for *her*," Angelo said.

"Unless she gets lucky and *learns* some things," Salvatore said.

"Some older brother *you* are," Gina said.

Salvatore lifted his wine glass. "This is nice."

"From Abruzzo," Angelo said.

"Long may the sun shine brightly on the sweet grapes in

Abruzzo." He drank.

"Speaking of prison, Sally, would you have preferred us to give you the visit to see Des Wigmore in Langnorton?"

"Me?" Salvatore said. "Naa."

"So your work is going all right?"

"What work?"

"You're not painting?" Angelo and Gina glanced at each other. "I thought you were."

"You got a wall you want done?"

"Please don't be flip," Gina said.

"I could be flop instead," Salvatore said. "Sorry. Sorry. But I'm OK."

"Because we could find you some work. You know that."

"What is it about 'I'm OK' that you're not hearing?" But then he lifted a hand to apologize for this shortness.

"I'm hearing that you're *not* OK," Gina said. "Since you ask."

Salvatore shrugged. "In which case I'm sure you know best because you're perceptive and wonderful. But whatever's not OK is nothing that would be fixed by going to Langnorton Open Prison to talk about holes in roofs."

"So it's not money."

"If I'm not buying paints and canvases, I don't need a lot. And before you ask, let me remind you that painting is an artistic pursuit and that artistic pursuits require artistic inspirations and when you ain't got no inspirations then you don't do no pursuing. Capiche?"

Gina sipped from her own glass. "Well, if you're free, I *was* thinking this might be a good time to give the kitchen an artistic coat of paint."

Salvatore smiled. "Papa would *love* that."

"It's sort of what he thinks you do anyway, isn't it?" Angelo said.

"Now now. I painted his portrait."

"Which he *did* love," Gina said. "Both the process and the result."

"Yeah?"

"You know damn well he did. And that's without having to hear the endless reports we got."

"You wouldn't let him talk while he was sitting for you, I gather," Angelo said.

"I needed him to keep quiet so I could concentrate."

"Or you'd paint him with his mouth open and his tongue out."

"I said that?" But the smile as Salvatore sipped made clear that he remembered saying it perfectly well.

Then he caught Gina's eye. When he'd done Papa's portrait there'd been talk of doing more, a whole series even. But before a second was begun Heather had buggered off with her new bloke. Not that he'd told the family that he now knew it was another man who'd broken up his happy home. Not that he wanted to talk about it now. He gave his head a little shake.

And Gina, lovely sensitive Gina, must have registered there was something he didn't want to talk about because what she said next was, "I think your painting Papa's portrait was part of what turned him around."

Salvatore drank more of his wine. "Papa turned around?"

"Became more alert. Became more connected with the family again."

"I thought that was Mama making him go to his gym."

"She wouldn't have been able to get him to do that if he hadn't been ready."

"No?"

"You, more than any of us, must know that Mama can't make anybody do anything they're not ready to do."

Mama's efforts to get Salvatore married had amounted to

little less than a crusade. She'd *thought* she'd taken Jerusalem when Heather moved in. Salvatore had thought the same, really believed it. Which was why Heather's abrupt departure had hit him so hard. Was still hitting him. He said, "Maybe Papa should paint *my* portrait. Maybe that would turn *me* around."

"I've only got Jaffa Cakes." Azaria set a tray on the glass-topped table that linked the two couches.

"I love Jaffa Cakes," Laurence said. "And it's a great place you've got here. Really interesting."

"Thank you."

The colours of the mugs harmonized with each other, the tray, and the colours in the room. Rosetta again felt the workings of an organized mind, but there was nothing wrong with that. She accepted her tea with enthusiasm. "You're a life-saver," she said.

"It's only English Breakfast." Azaria passed a mug to Laurence, who was sitting on the other couch.

"English and breakfast both sound good," he said.

Azaria sat by Rosetta and cupped her own mug with both hands. "Oh, I've been waiting for this," she said with a sigh.

"I mean it," Laurence said, continuing to look around the room from where he sat. "All the books and music and everything. It's very artistic." When this didn't elicit an immediate response he turned to the table and took two Jaffas.

Rosetta said, "It certainly doesn't look like a place you've moved to recently. Am I remembering it right? You haven't been here long?"

"Yes, a month and a half." Azaria stretched her feet out and slouched comfortably. She sipped from her mug with obvious pleasure.

"I'm sure I would still have boxes to unpack."

"Who's to say I don't?"

147

"I'd bet if we looked around we wouldn't find any," Rosetta said with a smile.

"So, you have a living room and kitchen down here," Laurence said. "What's the layout upstairs?"

"There will be no looking for unpacked boxes," Azaria said.

Laurence frowned, not understanding.

Rosetta and Azaria exchanged glances and raised their eyebrows, silently sharing an observation that Laurence seemed to be running on his own tracks. Azaria said, "There's a bedroom, bathroom and study upstairs. And an attic above that. And then a roof."

"Lovely," Laurence said.

Azaria drank again and worked her back into some of the cushions on the couch. Rosetta felt it was the first time she'd seen the beautiful woman relax. She looked smaller and warmer. Almost feline.

Less like a murderer?

Laurence said, "Where were you before you came to Bath?"

"Nottingham." It was said quietly and, after a moment, Azaria pulled herself back up into more of a sitting position.

"Is that where you were when you were married to Henry Daniels?"

"No."

The big man seemed oblivious to his host's body language, but it was clear to Rosetta that Azaria did *not* want to be put through part of the interrogation she'd just been through with the police. Yet Rosetta's impulse to protect Azaria was at odds with her curiosity about the answers that Laurence was getting, even the monosyllabic ones.

"So how long ago was that?" Laurence said. "Your marriage to Daniels, I mean."

"Not nearly long enough."

"And do you have a boyfriend now? Or a 'partner,' as they say?"

Ah, was that it?

But Azaria had had enough. "I'm in a deep, meaningful relationship with a boy named Matthew, but we're waiting till he's sixteen and doesn't need his mother's permission to be out at night. Jesus, Laurence, why are you asking me all these questions? Are you about to ask me out on a date?"

Laurence was so shocked at this that Rosetta thought she actually saw a ripple pass through his body. "Well, I, well, I thought I was just making conversation. Sorry if . . ."

"He's forgotten the kind of day you've had," Rosetta said. She felt an urge to pat Azaria's arm, so she did.

Azaria seemed grateful for the consideration. "I hate to be rude, but *honestly* Laurence."

"I never meant . . . I didn't think I . . . sorry. I really didn't . . . Look, I didn't mean to offend you or anything."

"I'm sure you didn't."

"Jaffa Cake?" Rosetta asked, holding the plate for her hostess.

Azaria accepted one on a serviette. "Thank you."

"Laurence?"

He looked like he was about to say "No," but then he took another two.

Azaria sipped again from her mug. "Henry was always a mistake."

"I am sorry," Rosetta said. "It has to have been a hellish day for you."

But before Azaria could respond, her doorbell rang. At the unexpected sound she jerked upright and spilled her tea. Her Jaffa Cake went flying.

Marie was not feeling at all well. The second vodka was a

mistake. A *big* mistake. She just hoped it wouldn't become a seriously embarrassing one. How awful it would be if she threw up in front of Rob. Or passed out. Or . . . or what? She didn't really know *what* she was feeling.

Perhaps she hadn't, after all, had enough orange left. Did orange lessen the power of the vodka? Was that why people drank them together? But was lessening the impact of the alcohol what people who drank wanted? That didn't make sense. But she certainly wished she had something to lessen the impact of *her* alcohol. Was this what being drunk was? People actually drank a lot in *order* to feel like this?

She should go home. At least in her own room she could lie down. The idea of lying down seemed like heaven. She stood up. But her thighs banged into the table and tipped her empty glass over. She'd forgotten to push her chair away first. Oops. And tipped her empty orange bottle onto the floor. Rob's drink was saved only because he managed to catch it. More oops. Marie covered her mouth so as not to be seen laughing at her oopsings. She dropped back onto the chair.

"Are you all right?" Rob asked.

"I don't . . ." But she shouldn't tell him how bad she felt. He'd think she wasn't used to drinking and not a university student after all and definitely not old enough to go out with him and show that bloody Jason. "I need to go home." But he'd want to know why. "Work."

"Of course," he said. "You were intending to do some work when you came in here, as I recall. So you've already given me the pleasure of your company for longer than you ever intended to. I hope our talking hasn't prevented what you have to do."

"No," Marie said. "Yes. Work."

"If you don't mind my saying so, Marie, you look a wee bit unsteady. Tell you what. I'm ready to get out of here too. What say I walk you home, to make sure you're safe. Is it far?"

Walk her home?

"For my peace of mind. OK?"

"OK." To know where she lived? Maybe he *did* want to go out with her. Maybe he would ask her on the way. "Yes," she said. "Yes."

Rob pulled the table out to make it easier for her to get up again.

"Sally, has something happened?" Gina asked.

Salvatore stared into her eyes. Did she know? Could she see? Sometimes it felt as if Gina could look into his very soul. She was special, this woman. He'd never met anyone who could *know* him like she did when she tried. He should never have let her get away. Angelo would have found another woman, some little wifey who would have done him just fine. He couldn't possibly appreciate Gina as much as she deserved. He didn't have the soul for it. Not that he should be thinking such things about his brother. His lovely steady brother who might not be artistic but had many other virtues. Many solid, steady *virtues*.

Salvatore drank from his glass. "Heather contacted me."

"After all these months? To say what?"

He gave a little snort. "She called to ask if I might want to exhibit in a gallery in Bristol."

Gina's eyes widened as she took in the statement. Then she said, "So Heather's in *Bristol.*"

"So it would seem. Not India, New Zealand, Brazil or Antarctica after all."

"And since she left, you had no idea where she was, where she's been?" Angelo asked.

"Not an idea of an idea, bro. I had so little idea that I began to expect that the police would show up at my door one day to ask if I had offed her. I even began to wonder if you guys thought maybe I'd offed her."

As Azaria wiped at her dress where she'd spilled her tea, her doorbell rang again. Rosetta said, "Would you like me to find out who it is?"

"I don't *want* to know who it is."

"Oh."

The bell went again. "It can't be anything good," Azaria said. "But yes, thank you, if you would." She got up, "I need to clean myself."

As Azaria walked to the kitchen, Rosetta followed as far as the intercom. She picked up the receiver and said, "Who is it?"

A male voice said, "Police. Open the door."

Rosetta wasn't quite sure what to do but Azaria called, "Who is it?"

"Someone claiming to be the police."

For a moment there was no further response from the kitchen. Then just, "Oh."

"Because someone claims to be police doesn't mean you should let them in the building. Why don't I go down?"

In Rosetta's ear the male voice said, "I *said* open the door."

"I'll be down in a minute. Have your warrant cards out for inspection, please." To Laurence she said, "Come downstairs with me."

"No one could *ever* think you'd do Heather or Salvia the slightest bit of harm," Gina said. "That's just foolish talk."

"OK, maybe not you guys, but think about it," Salvatore said. "One day I'm living with someone. The next day she vanishes off the face of the earth. No warning, no note, no forwarding address. Now what would Papa say if you put it to him like that?"

"At least now she's back on the face of the earth," Angelo said.

"Did she give you an explanation of any kind? Or an apology?" Gina said.

"She did say that she was sorry to have left so suddenly but that these things happen."

"What things?"

Salvatore took a deep breath. Might as well tell them. "Things like falling madly in love with someone else."

"*That's* what happened?"

"She ran off with another man."

"But she loved *you*," Gina said.

"Yeah, I kinda thought that myself."

"She was here. We all saw it."

Salvatore shrugged. "If she did, then it wasn't 'madly' and certainly not madly enough to keep her from having to follow the new object of her affections wherever he might lead."

"And the object of these affections led her to *Bristol?*" Angelo said. About fifteen miles from Bath, Bristol was four or five times larger but, for all its charms, more a place to live than a romantic or exotic destination.

"Takes a bit of the glamour out of the story, doesn't it?" Salvatore said.

"And having led her to Bristol, did he also keep her away from mobiles, postcards, fax machines and the internet?" Gina shook her head. "How incredibly thoughtless that woman is. How can she possibly justify treating you so badly, Salvatore?"

"I have to admit, saying 'these things happen' didn't quite seem enough to make it all better."

"I suppose she always did have a go-with-the-flow view of life," Angelo said.

"You can be a free spirit without abandoning all sense of responsibility as a grown-up," Gina said. "No, this is awful."

"I'll have a go-with-the-Flo view of life," Salvatore said, "the next time I meet a pretty Flo." He lifted his glass. "But this is more the flow I go with these days" He emptied it and poured himself some more, finishing the bottle. "Do you have another? Or some spirits?"

"You've drunk us dry," Gina said. She knew Salvatore would know she was lying.

And he knew she knew he wouldn't have drunk himself stupid in any case. But he smiled, and sniffed. "What a delicate bouquet this Abruzzo red has." He downed the wine in one go.

Angelo and Gina exchanged glances. Angelo said, "She said something about exhibiting?"

"Seems her new geezer is the decision-maker at some Bristol gallery."

"And she actually suggested that you might want to exhibit there? How very very *civilized*."

"That's not what *I* would call it," Gina said. "More like gross and insensitive."

"But will you do it, Sally?" Angelo asked.

"What? Exhibit?"

"Be civilized."

"No."

After a moment Gina said, "Even if it meant you might see Salvia again?"

Gina had the nub of it, as always. Salvatore sighed. For just a moment he wondered if there might be a way for him to prise his sister-in-law away from his brother. Could Angelo be less interested in her now that she was middle-aged? Some men lose interest in their women when they're no longer young. But Gina, she was more beautiful than ever, in her way. Older women's beauty is different but very real. Much *richer*.

But there was no way he and Gina could be together. Obviously. Not even by taking her somewhere off the face of the

Lunghi family's earth. God, what an ugly thought. Had he *really* considered, even for a moment, that he might break up the entire family in such a way? Maybe he was already stupid-drunk.

Even with Rob holding her arm, Marie had difficulty with the steps from the Assembly down to the pavement. "Careful," Rob said. "Nice and easy."

Steps shouldn't be hard. "Easy," Marie said.

"Now, which way from here?"

Marie turned to her left. They walked a few steps. Then she realized that she didn't have her handbag. "My bag." She jerked back toward the pub and nearly fell.

Rob managed to keep her upright and then held her bag up where she could see it. "I have your bag. And before we left we put everything of yours into it."

Marie saw the bag, suspended from Rob's shoulder. At least it was safe. That was good. "Good," she said.

They began to walk again. Slowly.

As Rosetta reached the ground floor, somebody outside started banging on the door with fists. "I'm coming," she called.

And the banger seemed to hear because he, or she, stopped.

Before she opened the door, Rosetta turned to Laurence. "Stand close behind me where they can see you."

"OK, but shouldn't we be leaving here anyway?"

"What do you mean?"

"Well, if they are the police it's not *our* business, is it?"

"Well, let's see just who it is, shall we? Ready?"

He nodded.

She opened the door. Facing her was D.I. Phillips. He and a woman in plain clothes behind him had their warrant cards up where they could be seen.

"*You,*" Phillips said.

"*You,*" Rosetta said.

Salvatore said, "Before Heather had Salvia, I'd never realized how wonderful babies are. I mean, I *know* you guys had your two but this was different. Maybe because I'm older now. Or maybe Salvia was just more *mine* somehow, even if she wasn't, biologically."

Gina and Angelo sat in silence for a moment. Then Angelo said, "There's nothing like 'em."

Salvatore lifted his empty glass. "To babies. Look. Can we talk about something else now?"

"Of course," Gina said. "Like what?"

"I've got a what," Angelo said.

Salvatore laughed, though knowing it wasn't that funny. He *was* a bit drunk. "What what, bro?"

"Should Papa really go to Langnorton Open Prison?"

"Why not?"

"I mean should he go *alone?*"

They all contemplated what the Old Man's going to Langnorton by himself meant. Would he go there by bus, or drive? Did he even know where it was?

But the Old Man was capable. He would get there. He might take longer than they would, or make more of a meal of it, but no one really doubted that he would get there. And get back.

Gina said, "In the morning I think we should review with him what he'll be trying to find out."

"What *is* he trying to find out?" Salvatore asked.

"Who Des Wigmore might have taught his technique to."

"How much *teaching?*" Angelo asked. "Drill some holes, connect the dots."

"Maybe there's more to it. Picking where to drill, for instance." Salvatore shrugged. "But if he's proud of it he might want to explain it all."

Gina said, "We should talk with Papa about how to find out about the prison's visiting procedures. Plus making sure ahead of time that Wigmore is willing to be interviewed. It won't help anyone to go there and be turned away."

"My sense of him from his wife is that he'll do whatever she wants him to," Angelo said. "We may need her to make a call, or sign an authorizing letter."

"It all needs to be arranged." Gina looked at the two men. "Do we feel Papa's up to it?"

"Maybe somebody *should* go with him," Salvatore said.

"He would hate that," Gina said.

"Unless . . ." Angelo held up a finger. "What if it was David?"

David was in front of his computer. He knew it was possible, even probable, that Lara would not be able to write to him again. Or even that she wouldn't anyway, whether she could get to her computer or not.

Yet how could he *not* believe that she would write if she could? After what had been said. "I *would* like to get to know you better if you'd like to get to know me," she'd written; "I'd *love* to get to know you better," he'd written back.

Use of the word "love" and putting it in italics had both been subjects of considerable deliberation. But he'd also wanted to send Lara a response as quickly as he could, so something would be waiting for her if she did get to her mail again. He'd "lost" a lot of time reading and rereading what she'd sent.

David was getting an idea of how Lara's household operated, how she had to work around her mother. But he had no idea how it was set up physically, whether Lara had any privacy, for instance. Did her mother always know when she was online? Could she even always look over her daughter's shoulder to see what was on the screen? Ooo, how yukky was *that* to think about.

Things like that argued against use of the word "love" and yet it had so many meanings and was used so freely that any of the other words that he tried in sentences seemed too cool. "I'd *like* to get to know you better"? No, no. Not even with the italics.

"Cool" had multiple meanings too, and was good in some ways, sure. David liked it when kids at school called him cool, even though he wasn't always sure they were being serious rather than sarcastic. But he did *not* want to take the slightest chance that his "coolness" might extinguish Lara's interest.

So he went for "love." And he went for the italics. She'd italicized him. Anything less in return . . . Well, David wasn't feeling anything "less." He felt everything "more." More and more and more and more.

So he'd sent it and consequences be damned. Better to have loved and lost . . . But why talk about losing?

And was he *really* talking about love?

Eleven minutes after he sent the message he finally sat down at the computer again. He had it in mind to keep himself busy. Open one of his ongoing projects. Or perhaps the less demanding option of playing a game.

Instead, he read Lara's last email one more time.

And something in it struck him that he hadn't really noticed before. Lara had written, ". . . when Marie's boyfriend saw me home . . ."

There were two things about this. Did Marie have a *boyfriend?* It wasn't common knowledge in the house if she did. Later in her email Lara named him, Jason.

Well, maybe the name Jason *had* come up, but it was certainly something to take Marie on with if she had a *boyfriend* and wasn't telling the family about him. What could this "Jason" be like that he had to be kept secret?

But the other point was that this Jason had *seen Lara home.* Why on earth would Marie's boyfriend have done that?

David reread on. Jason assumed that David and Lara were boyfriend and girlfriend too, but Lara had only not clarified the situation because ". . . he was talking away about other things like his plans and how great it is that you and I know stuff about programming computers and that he doesn't."

So was she saying that Marie had a boyfriend who wanted to learn about computers? Something about *that* felt wrong. And it was still odd that this boyfriend had gone with Lara to her home. David felt a pang of jealousy that Jason knew where Lara lived when he didn't.

And then there was a knock on David's door.

He was surprised by the sound, but he didn't jump out of his skin like the last time. He was much more together now. Much *cooler.*

He went to his door and opened it. And found his father standing outside. "Hi," David said. "I *am* fine. Really."

"Good, son. Good. May I come in?"

"OK. Just let me . . ." He minimized the email from Lara.

But his father didn't seem interested in what was on the computer. He sat on the edge of David's bed. "How are . . . things?"

"Fine. Really."

"So . . . the problems . . . earlier, I mean. They've been resolved?"

"Lara explained what happened. It's all cool."

"And so you're still friends?"

David's heart thumped suddenly, wanting to explode with how much more than *friends* he and Lara were, would be. But he leaned back in his computer chair and kept *cool.* "Yes."

"Good, good," his father said. "But, well, there's something else I wanted to ask you about."

"Fire away."

"We have a case—the one I was telling you about when we were at The Bell. Holes in the roof?"

"I remember," David said, though it took him a moment. "Crazy Coffee."

"Well, your grandfather is helping on it."

"He'll be glad about that."

"He'll be doing an important interview and we, your mum and I, we wondered if maybe you'd like to help him with making the arrangements."

"Me?"

"I'm not quite sure what it will involve. Maybe some things you can do by computer. Or the phone. You'd have to work everything out with him. But you like working on cases, don't you?"

There was nothing David liked better. At least there wasn't before today. "It wouldn't mean missing school, would it?"

"I'm not really sure."

"Because I wouldn't want to miss school." He was tempted to shout *Because of Lara who likes me!* but said instead. "What with my exams coming up and everything."

"Ah, your exams. Of course." His father frowned. "We'd temporarily forgotten them."

"Not that I'm worried."

"Mmm." His father still seemed thoughtful.

And Lara did have problems getting away from home out of school hours . . . plus, it would probably really impress her if he could say he was actually *working* on one of the family's cases. David said, "I could check it out with Grandpa. See if I can combine the two. Because he'd like me to show an interest in the business, wouldn't he? It could be on-the-job training."

"As long as it didn't take too much of your revision time."

"I wouldn't let that happen."

"And we do think your grandfather would like the teaching part of it."

"Would I get to be there for the interview itself?"

"Maybe. Possibly. It depends on what Papa wants and also whether it's allowed."

"Allowed?"

"The interview's a bit complicated. It's not in someone's house or office."

"Where is it?"

"Papa needs to interview a prisoner at Langnorton Open Prison."

David stared at his father. "Langnorton Open Prison?" He was suddenly confused. He didn't know how to react or what to feel. Intruded upon? Upset? What did they know? Were they reading his emails from Lara? Had they been *checking* on Lara and her family? He jumped up from his chair.

"David?"

"How dare you and Mum check the background of my girlfriend and her family?" he shouted. *"How dare you?"*

Rosetta led the way upstairs. She found Azaria on a couch in her living room, astonishingly having managed to change her clothes in the few minutes available. As people came in she rose, looking calm and relaxed. "So who do we have here?" she asked.

"This is D.I. Phillips," Rosetta said. "I don't know the other officer."

"Detective Constable Acorn," the female officer said. She was younger than Phillips and had a small red birthmark beside her left eye.

Although both officers held up their warrant cards, Azaria showed no interest. "Can I get you tea?" she asked. "Or coffee?

Or perhaps something stronger?"

"It's not a social call, Ms. Nolfi," Phillips said. "I'm here because I need to ask you some questions."

"Ask away."

"Down at the station."

"But I've only just come from there. I gave my statement to a D.C. Young. Surely she covered everything in that."

"I've read the statement you gave D.C. Young and some matters have arisen."

"Matters arising? Like at an AGM?"

"This is serious business, Ms. Nolfi."

"Am I laughing?"

"But before we leave, I want to know what Ms. Lunghi and Mr. East are doing at your flat."

"Drinking tea, having been invited in. Unlike yourselves."

"My understanding was that you were not well acquainted."

"I'm not well acquainted with you, yet you're here."

"Please don't be flippant."

"What I am is tired. *Very* tired, and I find it extremely difficult to see what on earth is to be gained by marching me back to your station to ask me questions when I am perfectly willing to answer your questions here."

"This is a murder enquiry, Ms. Nolfi."

"Although," Azaria said, "it is only classified as such until it is confirmed how Henry died and not because you actually know that he was murdered. Or was D.C. Young mistaken when she told me that?"

The policeman and the beautiful woman faced each other in a momentary stand-off, virtually a staring contest. It made Rosetta uncomfortable. "We ran into Ms. Nolfi after we left you, Inspector," she said.

Phillips turned to face her. "Ran into her?"

"On the steps outside the police station. Then, given that her ex-husband died today, we thought it civil to walk her home. Once here, she invited us in for a cup of tea."

"And Jaffa Cakes," Azaria said.

"We've not been here long and, frankly, I think you should show Ms. Nolfi some consideration."

"That would have been a lot easier if she had showed us the 'consideration' of explaining why she failed to mention that her husband was standing outside her house earlier in the day."

"I didn't bloody know he was there," Azaria said.

"By outside her house what do you mean exactly?" Rosetta asked.

Phillips turned to Rosetta. "Your own pictures show he was less than twenty yards away from where, according to *your* statement, Ms. Nolfi was standing. Is it *credible* that she didn't notice her ex-husband?"

"Was she asked to explain any of that?" Rosetta said. She and Phillips stared at each other. Then they turned to Azaria.

"I was not asked," Azaria said. "And, as it happens, my eyes aren't very good."

"Well, you *shall* be asked when we interview you again," Phillips said, "and I daresay we can get the results of your last eye test to see if they support your 'explanation.' But . . ." He turned to Rosetta again. "This is not a matter for either Ms. Lunghi or Mr. East. Therefore if you two would be so kind as to make yourselves scarce."

"Are you arresting Ms. Nolfi?" Rosetta asked.

"No."

Rosetta turned to Azaria. "Do you want to go to the station with these people?"

"Not really."

"Now just a damn minute," Phillips said.

"Do you have a lawyer, Azaria?"

"I came to Bath hoping I would never need to speak to any

member of the legal profession again."

"Because they can make you go to the station, but if you're tired or reluctant to talk to them for any reason, it can only be a good thing for you to be legally represented."

"Do you have anything to hide, Ms. Nolfi?" Phillips said.

"That's a stock question to make *you* defensive and it should be ignored," Rosetta said.

"Do *you* know a good lawyer, Rosetta?" Azaria said.

"I can get you one," Rosetta said. "Shall I?"

"Absolutely." Azaria was smiling now.

"May I use your phone?"

"Of course."

"I'm going to call my home and have someone there get you some legal representation." Turning to Phillips. "Shall Ms. Nolfi and her representative meet you down at the station?"

"Ms. Nolfi will be coming with us," Phillips said.

"Then," Rosetta said to Azaria, "answer none of their questions at all until someone engaged by the Lunghi Detective Agency gets there to help you."

"Detective agency?" Azaria said.

"My family's business." Rosetta dialled the Lunghis' home number. While it was ringing she wondered how she had moved so quickly from developing theories about Azaria as a murderer to wanting to defend her.

The answer was to be found in Phillips's eyes. A policeman with a murder to solve who thinks he has a plausible suspect can be *very* eager.

Marie and Rob managed to get across Lansdown Road and down the uneven paving stones of Hay Hill. More than once Marie had to lean heavily on his arm.

She'd expected to perk up in the fresh air. It's what happened as she walked home after their time in the Chameleon.

And then they came across the police and Auntie Rose and then the phone was stolen and then they followed as Auntie Rose chased after the thief.

"She didn't catch him though, did she?" Marie said to Rob.

"Sorry, Marie, but I don't know what you mean?"

"My Auntie Rose," Marie said. Then she remembered that Rob hadn't been with her. It was Jason. "Oh, sorry. I don't know what's wrong with me."

After a moment, Rob said, "Which way now?"

Marie looked where he was pointing. They were at the bottom of Hay Hill and the most direct route home was to cross the street and go down the Walcot Steps. But the idea of negotiating four irregular flights of stone steps was just too much to contemplate. Going around was longer, but leveller. And it might give her time to clear her head.

"Left," she said.

When the phone rang, Salvatore moved straight to the kitchen to answer it, so that neither Angelo nor Gina would feel the need to leave David's room. The panicky look on Angelo's face as he called for Gina to join them *was* a bit of a marker that having children wasn't all roses. Well, David was a good, solid kid. How bad could it be? "Lunghis," he said as he answered the phone.

"Sally?" The voice was Rosetta's.

"In the flesh. How you doin', sis?"

"Fine but this is a work thing."

"Can I handle it? Because Angelo and Gina are dealing with something with David."

"We have a new client who's about to be taken to Manvers Street. She's not under arrest but she needs legal representation."

"Tell her to confess. It'll save time all around." But when Rosetta did not respond, Salvatore said, "Who do you guys use these days?"

"I was thinking Grant Pullman, because it's a criminal matter. Gina will have his twenty-four-hour number in the office."

"I'll get it and call Pullman."

"If he's not available, have her suggest someone else."

"What's the client's name, Rose?"

"Azaria Nolfi."

"You what?"

Rosetta spelled it.

Salvatore said, "How long before she'll be at the nick?"

"We're at Cobham Court now. I assume the police came in a car." After a moment she said, "Yes, they came in a car."

"Will you be with her?"

"Hang on." Salvatore hung on. Cobham Court, did she say? Rosetta was back quickly. "I won't be going with Ms. Nolfi. The police think I may be a witness too and they don't want my evidence to be contaminated any further."

"A *witness?* Is this to do with that murder, Rose? That was Cobham Court, wasn't it?"

"That's all affirmative, Sally."

"You want me down there too, since you can't go?"

"If you don't mind. We don't want an unavoidable administrative mix-up at the police station to keep our client and her lawyer from finding each other, now do we?" Rose was obviously talking so that someone at her end could hear. A cop, presumably.

"I wonder," the Old Man said.

"What?" Mama put a cup of hot chocolate next to his armchair before lowering herself, and her own mug, onto a straight-backed chair at their little dining table. She'd sit in an easy chair too, but for her back. It had been irritating her today.

"I wonder, should I let you go to this Wigmore son?"

"*Let* me?"

"I mean go on your own. That's what I wonder if I should let."

"How do you plan to stop me, old man?"

"If you don't *want* company . . ." He picked up his chocolate and moved it to his lips. Then he blew on it and set it down again.

"Company you say now? That's different from 'let'."

"That's the same. Company is you're not alone when you tell a boy he's stupid about his mother."

"If you want to make company, I can't stop you."

"That's all right then."

They sat in silence for a few moments. Then Mama said, "And what about you and this prison?"

"What about me?"

"You could have company too."

The Old Man raised his shoulders in an exaggerated shrug. "Who needs it?"

"I didn't say need it, did I?" But after another moment Mama said, "Maybe I need it. Maybe I need to see this prison which is open."

He turned to her. "Why would you *need?*"

With a smile, because he'd fallen into it, she said, "So I can know where to come to visit you when they don't let you out again."

"Huh!" He took a sip of the chocolate. "Huh!"

Rosetta and Laurence watched D.I. Phillips load Azaria into the back of the police car. "I would *hate* that," Rosetta said.

"Being carted away by the cops?"

"I meant that thing where he puts his hand on your head as you're getting into the back seat."

"They do that to prevent—"

"I know what it's for, Laurence. But I can get into a car without some condescending copper making sure I don't hurt myself and sue."

Phillips's car backed out of Cobham Court.

"Where are you going now?" Rosetta said.

"Home, I suppose."

Rosetta didn't ask where that was. She didn't want to show interest in Laurence East that she no longer felt. "Me too, I suppose." She began to walk toward the corner.

Laurence was beside her. "You still haven't eaten."

"Oh yeah." Not that she felt hungry at the moment. There was something else on her mind. She didn't particularly want to extend her time with the big man, but . . . "Do you think we should stop in at the Committee Office?"

"Now?"

"It's not like it's midnight, Laurence. I just thought maybe people are still counting money in there."

"They'll have sorted all that out long since, don't you think?" Laurence was clearly without any enthusiasm for counting coins.

Nevertheless, a job on the committee was a job on the committee. "I'm going to look in," Rosetta said. "Especially since we're near The Bell anyway. But suit yourself."

Laurence already was. His attention had turned to the area of the street that was marked off by police tape. "Why do you think they've still got all that access restricted?"

"I suppose they're waiting for daylight to finish their search for things that might be connected with the death." The tape did cover quite a large area—the front of the Nazi's building as well as the fronts of the buildings on either side. Narrow passageways allowed the residents access to their front doors but they were out of luck if they wanted to take rubbish down to the basements via the outside steps similar to those in front of the buildings on Azaria's side of the road.

"I think it's more likely that Phillips just wants to *look* like he's doing something," Laurence said. "What an idiot."

Idiot? Rosetta hadn't been aware that Laurence felt animosity toward Phillips. Or was it just an expression of his dashed hopes for something with the beautiful Azaria? Neither notion moved her to comment.

They arrived at the corner of Walcot Street. Rosetta looked down the street toward home, although her intention was to go straight across to The Bell. Then she looked up the street.

And she looked again. Was that . . . ? Could that be . . . ? A woman up the street *looked* like Marie, walking unsteadily and being supported by a stocky man not much taller than she was.

Rosetta watched the couple make their way closer. She saw the woman stumble as she stepped down the kerb to cross Walcot Gate, a small street not far from Cobham Court.

It *was* Marie.

Behind Rosetta Laurence sighed. "I suppose it can't hurt to have a look in at the office."

"You go on."

"What?"

"I . . . I have something else to—" Rosetta watched in dismay as Marie attempted to walk in her direction. Even without the excuse of a street to cross, Marie was unsteady, often needing support from her companion. For what it was worth, the guy didn't seem to be rushing her or doing anything but help. Nevertheless, Marie was not even close to drinking age and if the guy was responsible for her condition . . .

"Isn't that your niece?" Laurence said.

"Yes."

"She's drunk."

Mr. Perception strikes again, Rosetta thought. "So it would appear."

"Is that her boyfriend?"

"I've never seen him before, but he might be."

"Bit old, isn't he?"

Marie stumbled over a paving stone near a streetlight and nearly fell. Her unknown companion managed to keep her on her feet by grabbing her by the waist and swinging her around. Rosetta and Laurence heard as the man said, "Whoopsie daisy."

Marie ended up facing in the wrong direction. As the man turned her back to the direction they'd been going, Marie laughed airily and said, "I'm *not* Daisy."

"He's not exactly a boy, is he?" Rosetta said.

"Hang on," Laurence said.

That's exactly what Marie's friend, boy or otherwise, was doing. Rosetta had seen enough. She walked quickly to where Marie was attempting to walk again.

"I think . . ." Laurence said, trailing behind.

Rosetta placed herself in front of her niece. "What the *hell* do you think you're doing, Marie?"

Marie blinked.

"Excuse me," the man with Marie said, "but who are you? Oh wait, let me guess. Are you Sally?"

"That's not Sally silly," Marie said.

"I'm her aunt," Rosetta said. "Who the hell are you?"

"I'm Rob Rafter. I'm afraid Marie had a bit more to drink than she could handle. I was seeing her home."

But before Rosetta could take Rob Rafter on about his responsibility for Marie's condition, Laurence clamped a massive hand on the back of Rafter's neck and said, "I just *bet* you were seeing her home, sunshine."

Salvatore was just about to leave when Angelo and Gina emerged into the kitchen. "How's the boy?" he said.

"A teenager in love," Angelo said. "Who'd do all that again?"

"There *are* good sides to all that stuff," Salvatore said.

Gina said, "You still probably go to clubs and try to pass yourself off as nineteen."

"Only in the dark."

"Ah, the *dark.*"

"Rhinestones look exactly like diamonds in the dark."

"Oh you're a bit better than a rhinestone even now, Sally," Gina said.

"You always did have a good eye," Salvatore said.

For a moment he pictured Gina when she was an art student, when he'd first met her, before she quit to marry. He'd been struck by her Italian good looks, though many people—perhaps even she herself—didn't recognize how beautiful she was. His eye had *always* been good, even if Gina's wasn't really. Not that he would ever tell her so.

"What?" Gina asked.

"*What* what?"

"You've been standing there with your mind off somewhere else."

"I have?"

"*Are* you all right, Salvatore?"

He shrugged. He really *must* get away from thinking about Gina in this way. "The Heather thing . . . you know."

Angelo said, "Did you find a lawyer for this client of Rose's?"

"One call, no problem. I've written the details down for you." He gestured to a bit of paper on the kitchen table. "Grant Pullman will be at Manvers Street soon, and I'm about to leave."

"And who is the new client?"

"Someone called Azaria Nolfi." Salvatore gestured to the paper.

"What kind of name is that?" Gina asked.

"The kind that is the ex-wife of the man they found dead in Cobham Court," Salvatore said.

"They think she killed him?"

"Apparently they're giving her first option."

"How did Rose find this client?" Angelo asked. "Has she been ambulance-chasing?"

"I have no idea how they got together."

"Maybe something from the pictures Rose brought that policeman here to see," Gina said.

"Could be."

"Where *is* Rose now?" Angelo said.

"She didn't say where she would be going next," Salvatore said. "She only said that she wasn't going to Manvers Street because the cops didn't want her there."

"She didn't say anything more about Nolfi?"

"Like what?"

"Like whether she can pay?"

"Our father would be proud of you, bro."

"I just asked." Angelo held his hands up.

"I'd ring her back to ask if her mobile hadn't been stolen." At that moment they all heard the door to the house open a flight below them. "Perhaps that's Rose now."

"Or," Gina said, "our errant daughter returning."

Several sets of footsteps began to climb the stairs, slowly.

"Has she brought everyone in the pub with her, d'you think?" Angelo said.

It was, indeed, Marie who stepped first into the kitchen. She gave everyone a big smile and wave. A moment later Rosetta appeared behind her, taking Marie by the waist.

"Nice timing, sis," Salvatore said. "Your new client has a new lawyer who should be on his way to Manvers Street now. I'm just leaving, to make sure they get together."

"Good," Rosetta said. "Thank you, Sally." She eased Marie to the side to make room for Salvatore to pass.

Marie was saying, "Hi Mum. Hi Dad. Hi . . ." She burst into laughter as she said, "Sally."

Whether to tell Lara or not was something David gave consideration to for a couple of minutes. But it was too curious a coincidence to omit, as long as he was careful how he presented it. No point, for instance, going through the confusion—that his first reaction was that it *couldn't* be a coincidence.

"You'll *never* guess," he wrote. "My parents have just been in my room to ask if I'll help my grandfather make arrangements to interview someone in *Langnorton.* Can you believe it? Totally out of the blue and a coincidence—nothing whatever to do with your dad. It's about a burglary at a coffee shop near here. But it did give me the chance to make sure they understand that someone being in Langnorton—or any prison—doesn't necessarily mean he's a bad person. And I'll say the same to Grandpa. And it also crossed my mind that maybe you could tell me what you have to do to arrange a visit there—what number you call and who you speak to. If you know, and if you don't mind. But I also spelled it out for my parents that much as I like to help them out with cases, there's no way I'm going to miss any school right now. I *said* it was because of exams. In fact, tomorrow I plan to be there early. About fifteen minutes? Miss Hamlish and the other teachers will think it's because I'm such a swat, but you know the real reason."

David considered whether to put the "you" in italics. Were italics going to be their own special graphic enhancement?

He decided to go for it, all out: ". . . but *you* know the *real* reason."

Laurence pulled out a chair and pushed Rob Rafter onto it. Rafter began to speak but Laurence said, "Just shut up."

"What is going on here?" Angelo asked, for Gina as well as himself.

Rosetta said, "We think this guy has given Rohypnol to Marie."

"You *what?*" Angelo said.

"That's ridiculous," Rafter said. "She got drunk. I was walking her home."

"Shut *up,*" Laurence said. "You don't want to make me tell you again." He was visibly angry and, given his size, extremely frightening. Rafter shut up. Everyone else in the room felt the impulse to do so too.

Except Marie, who didn't notice. "I'm sleepy. Really really sleepy."

"She is probably going to fall asleep," Rosetta said, "but to be on the safe side I think one of you should take her to A&E."

"What's been going on, Rose?" Gina asked with urgency.

"Laurence is in charge of security at Buick's. They keep track of potential troublemakers, including guys they think may try to use drugs on women. We met Marie and this . . . this *person* on the street. Laurence recognized him."

"I haven't done *anything,*" Rob Rafter said.

Laurence shaped up to threaten him into silence again but Gina said, "Let's hear what he has to say."

Rafter adjusted himself on the chair. "Thank you."

"Well?"

"I met Marie in a pub. We talked. I bought her a drink. She bought me a drink. Then she seemed really woozy and wanted to go home. I was ready to go so I said I'd walk with her, and it's just as well I did, because she was really gone, you know?"

He paused but if he thought anyone in the room would appreciate his generosity of spirit he was mistaken.

Rosetta said, "We first saw them coming down the street, just past Walcot Gate. Marie was *very* wobbly."

"I was taking her to her door," Rafter said. "End of story. What do you think I *am?*"

But it was obvious what people thought he was.

"First things first," Gina said.

"So can I go now?" Rafter said. He began to rise.

"Sit," Laurence said. "And keep your hands out on the table where I can see them." Rafter sat. He put his hands on the table.

"Does anybody know exactly what this drug does?" Gina said.

"I *didn't* give—" Rafter said.

"*Shut up,*" Laurence said.

Gina said, "Is there some way we're supposed to treat Marie?"

Rosetta said, "I'd think that giving her water would be good but I really don't know. So I think you and Angelo should take her to casualty. I'll stay here with Mr. Rafter. And perhaps . . . ?" She looked to Laurence.

"I'm not going anywhere," the big man said.

8

Angelo left to get one of the family cars from their garage in a nearby side street. After giving Marie's face a wipe with a flannel, Gina eased her to her feet and aimed her toward the stairs.

"I wanna go sleep," Marie protested.

"And sleep you will, sweetheart, you will," Gina said. "But we're going for a little ride first. And to do that you need to come down these stairs with me."

"Sleep," Marie said.

"One step."

Marie took one step.

"Another step."

Slowly they made their way to the bottom. Only the fact that Marie needed her mother for every step prevented Gina's rage from being turned on the young man upstairs. He might be sitting there afraid of Rosetta and her huge friend, but he should feel himself very lucky that he wasn't at Marie's mother's mercy.

"I'll call the police," Rosetta said.

"Good," Laurence said.

She picked up the kitchen receiver and began to dial a number, but Rob Rafter said, "Wait, wait, wait a minute."

Rosetta stopped and looked at him. "What?"

Rafter said, "Look, if I put my hands up to something, can't we just settle this like grown-ups." He lifted his hands. "I bought Marie doubles instead of singles, that's all. But I didn't mean anything by it."

"Didn't *mean* anything by it?" Rosetta repeated slowly.

"Hands on the table," Laurence said.

"Look, I got her drunk. But she bought drinks for me too."

"She's under age," Rosetta said.

"She said she was at college."

"She's obviously a schoolgirl."

"How do you tell these days? Honestly, I thought she was older. And she didn't say she wasn't."

Laurence clapped a hand on the back of Rafter's neck. "I said on the table."

Rafter returned his hands to the table.

"Out in the middle."

Slowly, Rafter complied.

Laurence said, "He's got stuff in his pockets that he wants to ditch before the police get here. I've seen it a hundred times."

"If anything's found in my pockets," Rafter said, "then someone here's planted it on me. Because when I came in this house I was clean as a whistle. In fact, I bet *you've* already done it. While you were roughing me up on the stairs."

"We'll just wait to see whose fingerprints are on whatever's in your pockets, shall we?"

"I could already have you for kidnapping and assault." He glared up at Laurence.

Laurence tweaked the young man's neck.

"Ow! Jesus, Jesus!" His hands flew to rub where it hurt.

"On the table."

"I've got to go to the loo. I've just come out of a pub, for Christ's sake. You don't want me to piss on the floor, do you?"

"OK," Laurence said. "Let's go to the loo."

"For—"

"Do you want to go or not?"

Rafter rose from his chair.

"But the jacket stays here."

Her arm around Marie's waist, Gina opened the door at the bottom of the stairs. Angelo wasn't out front with the car yet, but, seeing teams of people in the street clearing the mess left by the massive street party, she guessed that obstacles would need to be negotiated on Walcot Street until the clean-up was finished.

But no one would prevent Angelo from getting the car to them. There could be no man more devoted to the protection of his family than her husband. Too much, sometimes, if anything. Although how in this ridiculous day and age one could think any level of protection was "too much" was hard to say.

Gina looked at Marie, who was virtually asleep on her feet leaning against the doorframe. That her daughter, her baby, could be the target of a sexual predator was too much to take in. How could things like that *happen?* Fury rose in her so quickly that she needed the door for support for a moment herself.

But it was no good thinking about all that right now. Angelo would be here soon and it would speed things up if she could get Marie out to the kerb. Gently, Gina rocked her daughter back onto her feet and steered her toward the street. There was a lamppost there. It would serve as an alternative place for Marie to lean and to drift or sleep or whatever the hell she was doing.

They reached the lamppost without incident. But a moment later someone behind Gina said, "Marie?"

It was a young male voice. Gina turned to see a tall boy who did not look familiar. Who, indeed, looked very odd under the yellow light.

However, Marie had not responded to her name. Gina said,

"Who are you?"

"My name's Jason. I'm a friend of Marie's. And let me guess. You're Marie's . . . sister?"

"I'm her mother, Jason, and I'm not in the mood for childish bullshit."

"What's wrong with Marie, Mrs. Lunghi?"

"That's not really your business, is it?"

"No, you're right. Of course. Sorry. It's just that I care about Marie."

"Care about her tomorrow. At school? Do you go to school?"

"I'm in Year Thirteen."

"And isn't this a bit late to come visiting on a school night?"

"Actually, I'm not here to see Marie, Mrs. Lunghi."

Gina spotted Angelo's car approaching, at last. "Just passing through?"

"It's Marie's Aunt Rosetta I came to see."

"Rose?" Gina was confused now. "You're a friend of *hers?*"

"We've never met. Well, not properly."

Angelo pulled the car up and opened the passenger door. "I don't have time to deal with this now, Jason."

"Marie's aunt had a mobile stolen earlier this evening."

"Yes?"

"Well, I managed to get it back and I wanted to return it." He held a mobile up for Gina to see.

"I hope you appreciate," David wrote, "that I'm giving up my favourite dessert to chat with you." He pushed send.

After a moment, he received Lara's message, "What's your fave?"

"My grandma makes the most fantastic profiteroles."

"What are profiteroles?"

"Heaven on a plate. With cream and chocolate."

"Sorry you're making sacrifices for me."

"Would you like to try one? I *could* leave you, just for a minute, and get one from the fridge and bring it to you at school tomorrow."

"Don't *leave* me," Lara wrote. "Just eat one yourself and tell me about it. I fancy a virtual dessert."

David's heart fluttered.

Everyone in the kitchen heard a new set of footsteps on the stairs. "If that's the police, they've been quick," Laurence said.

"Maybe Gina forgot something," Rosetta said. "For Marie at the hospital?" She went to the landing, but what she found was a tall, fair-haired boy on his way up. Were Gina and Angelo expecting someone they forgot to mention?

"Ms. Lunghi?" The boy continued to climb.

"Uh huh."

When the boy reached the landing he stuck out a hand. "I'm Jason, a friend of Marie's. Her mother let me in because I have something—"

"Hang on, hang on," Rosetta said. "Who are you a friend of?"

"Marie, Ms. Lunghi."

"Well, Marie's not here now."

"I know. I just passed them outside. They were getting into a car."

"And Marie's mother let you in?"

"Yes, ma'am. I mean Ms."

"You do look familiar. What was your name again?"

"Jason. We haven't met properly but I was with Marie when your mobile phone was stolen."

Rosetta nodded. "The two of you followed along after me."

"We followed when you ran after the thief, although not quite at your speed."

"Why are you here now?"

"To return your phone. I managed to get it back and thought that I ought to bring it right over." He held Rosetta's mobile out for her.

"You have my phone?" Rosetta took the mobile and turned it over in her hands. "How is that possible?"

"It should be all right," Jason said. "I mean, I don't think it's damaged or anything."

"But how did you recover it?" Rosetta said. "Jason."

"Well, Marie and I were on the scene by the police tape when it was stolen. And the thing is, I happened to recognize the guy who took it."

"You *recognized* him?"

"I was pretty sure that I'd seen him around school. Not like he was a friend or anything, but I try to keep track of faces, you know? You never know when recognizing someone, or having met someone is going to come in handy. Case in point, eh? Networking . . . it's just something I do."

"You recognized the thief," Rosetta said, "and you didn't tell the police?"

"I was *pretty* sure who it was," Jason said, "but not certain. Although if he was who I thought he was, then I knew that he wasn't one of the really bad kids. He wasn't—well, he *isn't*—the kind of guy you'd expect to do something like that, you know? Mug someone. Run up and steal somebody's mobile. So I was really surprised. Anyway, I was going to mention it to Marie, or maybe to you—Marie said she was going to bring me home to dinner with you all, see. Only when we got to your door, she decided that with everything that had happened I shouldn't come up after all. At least not today. And then at the same time there was David's little friend with her letter and that whole thing. So I decided to check out whether I was right before I said anything, and see if maybe I could get the mobile back. And it turned out I was right and when I went to his house he said he didn't steal it to sell or anything, but that it was to help his girlfriend."

Rosetta was staring at Jason as he rat-a-tat-tatted away in front of her. "Help his girlfriend how?" she said when he finally paused.

"He said his girlfriend told him that you'd taken pictures of her earlier in the day, and that you threatened to get *her* in trouble with the police. So when they came back to Cobham Court later and saw the police there and saw you talking to them and saw the phone out, this guy thought the only way he could keep his girlfriend out of trouble was to nick it and run. So he did. Only he must have jostled the picture card out of it when he was getting away because when he and Emily looked, it wasn't there and he felt really stupid. And he's sorry if he upset you by taking it. And it's not the kind of thing he does— he's never been in trouble with the police and he's expecting good exam grades and all that—I wish *I* could have his grades, I really do. Although I haven't done the work, so I deserve whatever I get. It's a really nice mobile, though. I'm sure you can get another card for it."

"Stop," Rosetta said.

"Sorry. I'm a bit nervous."

"I did take pictures of some aggressive girls at the Cobham Court barrier. One of those was this Emily?"

"Emily *is* a bit pushy," Jason said. "But Nigel likes her a lot."

"Well, thank you for the return of the mobile, Jason. I'm going to have to think about all this when I have a chance. But I do appreciate your getting it back and bringing it to me."

"That's quite all right, Ms. Lunghi," Jason said. "My pleasure, really." He smiled.

After a moment, Rosetta felt obliged to say, "Look, would you like a cup of tea or something before you go?"

"That would be great. Thank you."

"Well, come in then." Rosetta stepped back.

As Jason followed her into the room he said, "So is something wrong with Marie? When I saw her downstairs with her mum, she looked pretty out of it."

"She . . . isn't well," Rosetta said. "How do you take your tea?"

"Milk and one sugar, please, Ms. Lunghi."

"Do have a seat." Rosetta pointed to the empty chairs at the end opposite to where Rob Rafter sat with Laurence standing behind him.

But instead of sitting, Jason stared at Rafter. There was a shocked expression on his face.

"Jason?" Rosetta said.

"What is *he* doing here?"

"Do you know him?"

"Not personally, but I know what he *does.*"

"Which is?"

"Around school they call him Rob E."

Everyone turned to face Rafter.

"He sells pills," Jason said.

"Bollocks," Rafter said.

"Not to me or anything," Jason said, "but I talk to people, you know? I mix. And I've heard some of the sporty guys talk about him and they pointed him out a couple of times."

"He's making it all up," Rafter said.

"Is *that* what's wrong with Marie? He's given her something?" Jason said. "Oh *Jesus*. What have you done to her, you scum?" He moved around the table.

"Nothing, *nothing.*"

Laurence moved into Jason's path. "We've called the police and they'll be here any minute." He turned back to face Rafter. "Let's see how the law plans to deal with him before we start improvising."

The doorbell rang.

Rafter jerked, as if he'd been hit.

Rosetta said, "I'll go down and let them in." She headed for the landing.

"Hands on the *table*," Laurence said sharply.

"All right, all right," Rafter said. He put his hands down but then suddenly pushed the table with his feet, catching Laurence above his knees with a corner. The big man rocked backwards.

With Laurence momentarily out of the way and Jason partially blocking the corridor that led to the bedrooms, Rafter ran for the landing. Rosetta was already on the stairs that led down to the street, so Rafter ran up instead.

The Old Man held a small plate in his hand. He was headed for the kitchen, to put the plate in the washing-up bowl. It was the least he could do after finishing this profiterole that Mama surprised him with. "Good," he said. "Good, good, good."

"I'm glad you like," Mama said.

"Good you didn't give them all away."

"For the Sunday dinner that never happened?" Mama sighed.

Then they both heard noises. The sounds seemed to be footsteps on the stairs. "You hear?" the Old Man said.

"Who *runs* up the stairs? I can't think."

The Old Man shook his head. No one ran up stairs these days, though you *could* do such a thing instead of the gym and save the fees. The children, back when they *were* children, they raced up and down and up again. But nowadays even the children's children weren't children anymore. Not adults either, so who knew what David and Marie were. "Huh!"

Then whoever it was arrived at their landing and hit the door.

The Old Man and Mama looked at each other, Mama with a puzzled frown.

A moment later the handle turned and the door flew open. A stocky young man rushed in. *"How do I get out of here?"* he shouted. He slammed the door behind him and fiddled till he found some way to lock it. *"How do I get out?"*

"Who are you to run into our flat in such a way? With your shouting," the Old Man said.

"Don't mess with me, grandpa. Just tell me how I get out of here. There must be a back door or a fire escape or *something.*"

The truth was that the flat *did* have an emergency exit—through the living room window and onto a ledge and the flat roof next door, in case of fire. Not that anyone ever used it. Not that such an intruder as this was going to use it either. Who was he, this man? A burglar?

"You want out of here? Go back the way you came, unless you want to jump and be a splat on the street." The thought of the dead man who'd already been found today flashed into his mind. Perhaps that's the way he'd died, jumping out a window because he was a burglar and didn't know about a flat roof next door.

There was more noise on the stairs now.

The intruder grabbed an upholstered chair and threw it aside in frustration. He looked around the room.

The Old Man glanced too and saw Mama retreat toward the kitchen. For a knife perhaps? No, she looked frightened. And that was *not* tolerable. Not in *this* house.

Behind the intruder someone tried the door but couldn't get in because it was locked.

The sound made the intruder jump away from the door. By luck or accident he headed for the window that would allow his escape. He reached out to push the Old Man aside.

But the Old Man grabbed the intruder's arm and pulled it. He also stuck out a leg. It wasn't organized, or trained, but one way and another he pitched the young man over onto the floor.

By holding on the Old Man fell on top. The two men lay there for a moment from the shock of it all.

The Old Man heard the door to the flat open and Mama shout, "Rosetta! Save your father!"

But Rosetta said, "Are you sure it isn't the other guy who needs the saving?"

The thought of his grandmother's profiteroles combined with Lara's encouragement sent David straight to the kitchen.

He couldn't believe his luck. No one was there. He'd been ready to run the gantlet of parents, aunt and uncle, grandparents, even his sister, all asking questions about this Lara. What, a new girl in your life? What's she like? Are you going out together now? When's the wedding?

Not that David had any intentions of getting bogged down trying to answer such questions. And he certainly had no intentions of stopping for a chat, even if he had to be rude. He'd get a plate, get a profiterole—two if there were two—and go back to his room while doing the teenage thing. "Leave me alone, leave me *alone!*"

Instead, he'd struck lucky. He pulled a plate from the cupboard and went to the fridge.

But then there were footsteps on the stairs. *Lots* of them. Someone—a man whose voice he didn't recognize—called "Did you get him?" and someone else called something that seemed to be affirmative. David couldn't remember so many people being on the stairs at the same time before. Some steps seemed to be coming up. Some seemed to be coming down. How many people were *out* there?

A profiterole sat on a plate at the front of the fridge. He grabbed it but by the time he'd closed the door, his aunt was in the kitchen. But David had no sooner said, "Hi Auntie Rose," than she was followed by two police officers, one male and one female. The man was the copper who'd been in the flat earlier.

Then behind them, Auntie Rose's big friend who ate all the food earlier in the evening came in pushing a funny-looking man ahead of him. The huge man had the funny-looking man in an armlock and forced him to a chair while behind them a tall blond-haired boy entered the kitchen.

David stood wide-eyed as these people spread themselves around the kitchen, only to be joined by his grandfather and, finally, his grandmother.

"What . . . what's going on?" David asked.

"I was only going to rob her," the funny looking man in the chair said. "Just steal stuff. I'm not a pervert."

"You see, everybody," Mama said. "David likes my profiteroles too."

9

"Fighting in the house, and *poor* Marie. Who would think such horrible things could happen?" Mama sat with a cup of tea. "I blame this awful Nation Day."

"How can you blame *that?*" the Old Man said. He too sat but he was resting rather than eating or drinking. Tired and ready to go back upstairs to bed, after all the carry-on. Otherwise, he would have gone with the police and this Jason to Manvers Street to give his statement. But capturing the villain single-handed was enough for one day. He could give his statement tomorrow. The nice policewoman said they would send some-one.

"Of *course* the Nation Day causes all the trouble," Mama said. "I'm sorry, Rose—and you too, Laurence—but such a Day overexcites everyone with noise, and then they drink too much. It's no surprise if everything goes crazy."

"You too could be less noise," the Old Man said.

"Well, anybody *knows* it's wrong to upset what people are used to, like to miss a dinner you always have on a Sunday. How can that be right?"

The mobile rang.

Rosetta jumped up and took it, hoping it was a call about Marie. Mama, Papa and Laurence all listened as she said, "Angelo, we've been so worried." Then she said nothing.

Mama said, "What? What's happened? How is our Marie?"

"Give her the time to find out, old woman," the Old Man

said. "Be patient."

"Should I have been patient unlocking the door upstairs? Taken my time while you fight with that bad man? How would you have got on then with your wrestle?"

"He was under control. I could have waited for you to unlock. And make yourself a sandwich first. Huh!" The Old Man made a muscle.

Mama sipped. "So do they teach lying on top of people at this gym of yours? No wonder it's so popular with the young ones." But she patted his hand.

Rosetta said, "That's great. I'll let them know." She hung up.

"So let us know," the Old Man said.

"Marie's fine. They'll keep her in overnight, for observation, but this drug just makes her sleep. It's extremely unlikely that there will be any ill effects."

"Such a relief," Mama said. "I hope they throw away the key."

"She should be back to her old self tomorrow, although it's very unlikely that she'll remember anything that happened or even understand why she's in a hospital bed when she wakes up."

"She won't remember?" the Old Man said. "How can we know what happened if she doesn't tell us?"

"It's the way this drug works, Papa. It causes an amnesia, especially when it's taken with alcohol."

"Alcohol? Marie? But that can't be right," Mama said.

"The man Papa tackled bought big drinks for her. But I'll call Salvatore. Maybe he'll be able to find out more since he's already at Manvers Street."

"That blond boy, Jason. He seemed nice."

"He was certainly upset when he realized that Marie had been out with Rafter."

"I'm sure Jason wouldn't force Marie to have alcohol," Mama

said. "We should thank him. Invite him for dinner on Tuesday."

"Marie doesn't want your foolish matchmaking," the Old Man said.

"Who makes matches? This is thanking."

"If you're thanking people," Rosetta said, "then you should thank Laurence here."

They turned to Laurence who had been served with a plate of desserts. Mama said, "You're so quiet."

"I don't like to interrupt family conversation. But I must say, Mrs. Lunghi, these are the best profiteroles I've ever tasted."

"Such good taste you have," Mama said. She smiled at her joke and looked around to see if the others had heard it.

"Tell us again why we thank," the Old Man said.

"It was Laurence who recognized Rob Rafter first," Rosetta said.

"You *knew* this Rafter?"

"I knew him as an undesirable at the club I work in."

Rosetta said, "It's because Laurence recognized Rafter that we brought him back to the flat."

"Well, thank you Laurence," Mama said. "Thank you to make it possible for my husband to tackle and remove this Rafter from the streets. Would you care to come to dinner with us on Tuesday?"

"I'd be delighted to, Mrs. Lunghi. Thank you."

The Old Man said to Rosetta, "Angelo, did he say when he and Gina come home?"

"Gina's staying overnight at the hospital to be with Marie when she wakes up. Angelo was going back up to see them, and then he'll come home, to be here for David."

"And where is our David?" The Old Man looked around. "This computer work he said he had to do, how long can it take?"

★ ★ ★ ★ ★

"You will *never* believe," David had written to Lara, "all the *amazing* things that have been going on here." He'd considered suggesting it was all just a day in the life of private detectives, but then thought better of it. A day like this would be hard to live up to if he and Lara were going to *get to know each other better* . . .

Mama stood up.

"You're going somewhere?" the Old Man said.

"I go up to sleep. You too should sleep."

"Not wait for Angelo?"

"Who knows when he gets back. He tells Rose that Marie is all right. What else matters when tomorrow there is a day?"

"Ah, you have the bad son to teach how to treat his mother."

"And you must arrange to go to prison. Make sure they don't lock the door behind."

The Old Man nodded. "We go up."

"Sleep well, Papa, Mama," Rosetta said.

"And, Rosetta should have some time with her giant friend without her father at the table," Mama said.

"It's not her father who marries her to all and sundry. Huh!" The Old Man rose.

"Don't mind my husband," Mama said to Laurence. "He has a mouth when he gets tired but it doesn't inherit."

"Oh," Laurence said, unsure what response was wanted. "OK."

"But you we see again for dinner on Tuesday."

"Thank you." Laurence rose.

"If not before," Mama said. "No, don't get up for us to leave."

"I'd better get on my way too," Laurence said.

"No no, sit. Have a drink. Rose, make your friend some tea. Or wine."

191

"Mama!" Rosetta said.

"I go. I go." Mama headed for the landing and the Old Man followed. At the kitchen door she waited for him to pass her and then closed the door behind them.

Rosetta said, "It's not always an advantage to have family so close by."

"They're lovely," Laurence said. "However, I am going now."

"It is late."

"Actually I want to look in at the club."

"Is it open on Sundays?"

"Not always but tonight's a private party. I'm not on duty, because of the early start for Nation Day, but I want to look in and make sure everything is as it should be."

"The responsibility of being responsible . . ."

"Exactly."

Rosetta stood, but Laurence did not head for the door immediately. The moment was slightly awkward. He said, "Are you coming out? You did say you wanted to look in at the committee room. We could do that now, although I wouldn't want to stay to count money."

"I think I want to be here when Angelo gets back. He should be told about everything that's happened."

"Of course."

"Marie may well be all right but it was hard to tell on the phone whether Angelo is."

"Did something happen to him?"

"Nobody hit him on the head but what happened to Marie could have been truly awful."

"But it wasn't."

"No," Rosetta said. Through the day Laurence had repeatedly shown himself unable to understand other people's feelings. Despite his virtues. Do things like that ever change? Suppose he had a daughter of his own. Would he understand then what Angelo might be going through? The idea of having a daughter with Laurence made her flush. "It wasn't."

When Angelo finally got home Rosetta met him at the top of the stairs. "What?" he said.

"Just your welcome committee."

"You Nation Day people take the committee thing very seriously."

Rosetta hugged her brother. "I'm so sorry about Marie."

"I don't think I'll ever go to sleep at night again before I know she's safe." Angelo came into the kitchen and noticed a half-filled plate and a half-empty cup of tea on the table. "Eat. Don't let me interrupt."

Rosetta glanced at the food, having forgotten it. "I'm not really hungry now." She picked up her plate to clear it.

Angelo grabbed the mug to help. It was cold. "What's wrong?"

"Nothing. Everything." Rosetta scraped the food into the bin.

After a moment Angelo asked, "What happened to Rafter? The police take him away?"

"We called them but when they got here Rafter tried to run for it."

Angelo straightened. "The bastard didn't get away, did he?"

Rosetta shook her head. "Papa tackled him."

"Ex*cuse* me? *Papa* tackled him?" Angelo took a glass from a cabinet. "Want some wine?"

"Just a little."

He took out another glass and poured from a bottle in the fridge. "Papa chased Rafter down the street and rugby-tackled him?"

"Well he *does* train at the gym."

"Was he demonstrating what he would have had you do to that guy who stole your phone?" Angelo sat next to his sister at the table. "Here's to a safe family."

They clinked glasses.

Rosetta said, "Rafter knew the police were coming but when he heard the doorbell downstairs, he ran upstairs and broke into Mama's and Papa's flat. We all followed but when we got there, we found Papa on top of him on the floor."

Angelo tried to picture his father atop Rob Rafter. "I miss all the fun."

"The police took him away. I rang Salvatore at the station to ask him to find out whatever he can about Rafter while he's there. The police will send someone to take Papa's statement tomorrow but that Jason boy went along with them tonight."

"What Jason boy?"

"Marie's friend? The one who returned my mobile?"

Angelo looked blank.

"He came up after you left. Said Gina let him in?"

"Tall, fair-haired?"

"That's him."

"I remember now. He was there when I picked up Gina and Marie."

"Well, Jason managed to recover my mobile. He was returning it to me."

"He *recovered* your mobile?"

"He recognized the kid who stole it, so he went to the kid's house and got it back."

"Well, well, well." Angelo sipped from the wine.

"And Jason also recognized Rafter as a pill-pusher who hangs around at the school."

"Jason recognizes? Do we take this at face value?"

"Oh I think so."

"OK." But Angelo shook his head slowly. "We know they exist, these predatory Rafters. I just never thought we'd have one in our own kitchen."

"Mama's invited Jason to dinner on Tuesday as a thank you.

She's invited Laurence East as well."

"The big guy?"

"He recognized Rafter too."

Angelo considered. "Jason and Laurence both recognize a pill-pusher?" He spread his hands. "Customers?"

"They both convinced me they're not," Rosetta said.

Angelo shrugged. "Forgive me if I'm not in a trusting frame of mind." He sipped again from his wine. "If your big friend comes to dinner, we'll need to make twice as much food. Is Mama pairing you off with him?"

"Mama would pair me off with Jason," Rosetta said, sipping from her own wine.

"Jason is at school with Marie, I take it."

"I think so."

"You could help him with his homework."

"It's not going to happen," Rosetta said.

"He should do his own homework?"

"Ha ha."

"So you're not thinking that way about the big man either?"

"Thinking, yes. But not about Laurence."

"About what then?"

"That I may move out. To my own flat."

"Really?"

"At my age, who still lives at home?"

"Most people these days, it *seems*," Angelo said to his younger sister.

"What do you think about me getting my own place?"

Angelo considered. "I think it's a good idea. But don't quote me to Mama."

Rosetta offered her glass again. They clinked. "Thank you," she said.

"And how is David?"

"I haven't seen him for hours."

After exchanging glances, the siblings rose and carried their glasses down the corridor to David's door. From outside they heard the sound of computer keys being tapped.

"At least he's alive," Angelo said quietly.

"It's so late. Should we tell him to pack it in?"

"He's in love. *You* tell him to pack it in."

"I don't know much about love," Rosetta said.

"Your day will come."

"You think?"

"But this day is David's." After a moment Angelo said, "Maybe we should knock, tell him it's a school night, then go away so he can tap in secret, make it wicked, give him a complaint so he can be a teenager."

But Rosetta didn't get a chance to comment on her brother's parental strategy because the door they were whispering outside of suddenly opened. David looked from one to the other of them. "What?"

"Just making sure you're all right," Angelo said.

"I'm fine."

"Good."

"Good," Rosetta said.

David began to shut the door but stopped. "Are there any profiteroles left?"

Rosetta went to the living room after Angelo finished his wine and turned in. She was tired—who wouldn't be after her day?—but she wasn't sleepy. She was excited at the prospect of change. Given that she'd never seriously thought about moving out of the family house before, the idea felt deliciously right. Something deep inside of her was satisfied by it.

She considered getting herself another glass of wine to celebrate her decision, but decided instead to go out for a walk. It was a lovely warm summer's night. And she was a strong, independent woman. If she felt like going for a walk, why not?

However, when she went out the door Walcot Street was not the quiet place it usually was on a Sunday night. The stage was long gone but there were still a lot of people about, not least those who were sweeping and bagging the detritus of the day, piling it for collection. It's not that the street would show no signs in the morning of what had taken place the day before, but although it might look like the aftermath of a riot, there would be nothing left to interfere with Walcot's business-as-usual.

Rosetta turned toward Cobham Court and began to walk. There was no reason why moving out, to her own little place, should interfere with her business-as-usual in the family. Salvatore had lived on his own for years. Was he less a part of the family for that?

Coming up on her right Rosetta saw the lights outside Buick's. She thought about stopping in to say hello to Laurence, having a look at this nightclub on her street that she'd never been inside. All she knew was that the stairs from the entrance led down to basement level.

Why had clubs never been her scene? There was no good answer to the question. They just weren't. And were all nightclubs in Bath subterranean? One had even been set up in disused public toilets below a traffic circle known to residents as Bog Island, though it was closed now.

And the city's oldest tourist attraction, the Roman Baths, were below street level too, even though they weren't designed that way. Two thousand years' worth of rubble and unbagged detritus had raised Bath's street level outside the hot springs by a dozen feet. Still, nightclubs and Romans and basements . . . it all smacked of orgies and decadence. And pill-pushers like the despicable Rob-E.

No, Rosetta wasn't really much interested in seeing Buick's.

Or Laurence. Laurence . . . no doubt a good-enough-hearted man in his way, but whatever his physical appeal, his lack of sensitivity to feelings meant he was not going to be the man for her.

So Rosetta walked past Buick's without stopping. And on Monday she would leave him a message there with some excuse, asking him not to come to dinner after all on Tuesday. Attending a family dinner would give Mama false hope. The family could send him a thank-you card. And Azaria's mobile number . . .

Farther up the street Rosetta came to the corner with Cobham Court. A policeman still stood guard at the taped-off area but now there was a police car there too, for him to sit in. And was that a second officer in the car? It was. Good, someone for the guard to talk to. Perhaps a patrol officer who found Bath on a Sunday night to be so quiet he could park for a while.

When next she came to The Bell, Rosetta decided to check the Nation Day committee room. Better late than never, although there was no chance, surely, that the count would still be going on. There wasn't *that* much money, was there? However, much of it was in small change. And even if not many people had returned to complete the job, Rosetta felt that she would like to be able to say that she had, eventually, come back to offer help.

She passed through the archway and walked around the back. There was still some noise from inside the pub but the outside area had been cleaned up and there was no one there.

Rosetta passed the empty picnic tables and benches and rounded the corner that led to the committee room. Not surprisingly, the two windows were dark. OK, duty fulfilled. But just as she was about to turn back to the street, she heard a noise. It was a sharp bang. Nothing subtle.

She stopped, wondering at first if she really had heard what she thought she'd heard. But this was not a day on which she was minded to doubt herself. If she'd heard a noise then there'd been a noise. But what could it be?

She stood still, waiting in case it was repeated. Meanwhile, she reviewed what she'd heard and where it had seemed to come from. Definitely from in front of her, not behind. But might it have come from above rather than from within the committee room? The Nation Day HQ nestled against a wall that was below the gardens behind the Paragon, a long crescent of buildings on a steep hill above Walcot Street. The direction was right, but the sound had seemed closer.

So Rosetta approached the committee room. For a few moments she listened carefully outside the door and heard nothing. She went to the first window. Nothing. Then the next. And outside this window she did hear more sounds, quiet ones this time, from activity inside.

She frowned as she thought about what might be going on in there. It *needn't* be anything bad. And yet what could be happening in the darkness that was legitimate activity?

She edged back to the door. Gently she tried the handle. It resisted firmly. Locked.

She stepped back to think. One explanation came to her quickly. That there was not one person inside but two. Perhaps a couple seeking a special place to celebrate the end of this year's Nation of Walcot.

With a little smile Rosetta considered who they might be. It was a novel way for her to be thinking about the members of the committee. Which of them might be up for a jape like *this?* Hmmm.

At least one of them would have to be a key-holder. She tried to remember who had keys to the room. Barbara, of course, as Chair, but not *Barbara,* surely. Mind you, there were those who were snide about the amount of time she spent with Alan Carter. But there were other possibilities. Stephanie? Were her ambitions to replace Barbara partly because she wanted a little domain to call her own?

And then, as Rosetta stood before the door, there was a click.

She stepped back, preparing for the unexpected opportunity to have her speculations answered definitively. How do you greet people in a situation like this? As if nothing unusual has happened even though their hair is everywhere and there's a glow in their eyes? Or with her mobile out, ready to take a picture?

The handle of the door turned, slowly.

Thanks to Jason, Rosetta had her mobile back and she'd reinstalled its picture card. She opened her handbag and found it. Naughty to be thinking of doing such a thing, really. But she was ready if she decided she wanted to.

But the man who emerged from the committee room was alone and he was a complete stranger. About five-eight, fiftyish and slim, he wore grey trousers and a long-sleeved grey shirt. One of the sleeves looked dusty. He carried two soft bags like the one Papa used for his gym equipment. Both bags sagged as if filled with heavy things.

"Evening," the man said.

"Er, hello."

"It's been a cracking day today, hasn't it?" The man gave a polite smile and moved to pass her.

"Excuse me," Rosetta said, "but what were you doing in the committee room?"

"There was a problem with the electrics."

"And you fixed it?"

"I tried, but I'll have to come back." The man carried on.

But Rosetta followed. "Hang on a minute. When will you come back?"

"Oh tomorrow, first thing."

"And you are?"

"Tony. Tony Brown."

"Who was it who told you about the problem?"

The man didn't stop, but he looked back as he said, "I didn't get his name. Jack, maybe? But I'm not good with names. It was on a mobile and it wasn't very clear."

"And who do you work for?"

The man stopped and turned. "Look, lady, it's late. I'm tired. I tried to fix it—at least to make do till the morning, but I couldn't. I'm sorry if I can't give you chapter and verse about who called me tonight, but it's been a long day. Walcot Nation and all that, y'know? So cut me some slack."

Rosetta knew all about how long the day had been, but she felt something wasn't right. Something specific. "Just tell me your mobile number then."

"And my address and my shoe size and my children's middle names? Get a life, lady. I'm tired and these bags are heavy."

And then she got it. This man had unlocked the door but had *not* relocked it when he came out of the committee room. That could have been a tired oversight, of course, but . . . She said, "It's just that Rosetta is usually the one who calls people in for repairs."

"Ah," Tony Brown said. "*Rosetta* . . . that was her. I must be getting old, but I did tell you it was a bad connection."

She put up a hand.

"What *now?*"

"*I* am Rosetta, Mr. Brown, or whatever your name is."

"Tony Brown" fixed her eyes for a moment. Then he turned around and headed for the gate.

"Stop. I want to see what's in those bags," she called.

"Tony Brown" began to run.

For the second time in the day Rosetta pursued a fleeing

man. At least this time she had her mobile. She flipped it open as she ran.

Although "Tony Brown" was not as quick as the lad hours earlier, he was not slow, even with the bags. He got clear of The Bell and was headed up Walcot Street before Rosetta caught him. She grabbed his collar.

He did not struggle. He turned and squared up to her. "You do *not* want to get in a ruck with *me*, young lady."

"I don't *want* to get in a ruck with anyone," Rosetta said. She stepped back, lifted the mobile and snapped.

The automatic flash blinded "Brown" for a moment. "Jesus," he said.

"But I'm not just going to let you waltz off with whatever you've taken."

"Brown" dropped the heavy bags on the pavement. "Give me the mobile, lady."

Rosetta stepped farther away and put the mobile behind her back but before she could turn to run "Brown" took her arm in a powerful grip.

But then behind her and not far away a voice called, "Rosetta? Rosetta is that you? Are you all right?"

"Tony Brown" looked past her shoulder. His face showed shock. He turned and bolted. He was *much* faster without his heavy bags.

"Are you awake?" Gina said when Angelo answered the mobile.

"Has something happened?" Angelo asked.

"No no. I just couldn't sleep. Do you mind?"

"Of course not."

"Marie's fine."

"Good."

"Do you remember her, when she was a baby?"

Angelo rubbed his eyes. He'd been dreaming of what? Of a

bowling alley on its side. Could that be right? "Of course," he said. He sat himself up and sipped from the water by the bed.

"I mean the way sometimes when she was tired she'd fall asleep any old way. Arms out here, legs out there, on her back or her tummy, whatever."

And then an image of baby Marie came into Angelo's mind. Splayed on a cushion on the couch. But she did that a lot, falling asleep in odd positions. He and Gina would call to each other to point them out. Were there some pictures? "I do remember."

"She's just like that now. You could drape her over a barrel and she'd stay put."

David had always been finicky about how and where he slept. "I miss you," Angelo said.

"I miss you too."

When Rosetta turned toward the voice, she half-expected to see the huge form of Laurence running toward her. Instead, it was a police officer in uniform. Felix McCough.

When he got to her he said, "I saw the flash. Then I saw it was you. Still taking your pictures, eh?"

"That man," Rosetta said, pointing to the fleeing figure in the distance, "he robbed the Nation Day offices."

"He did?" McCough looked up the road and squinted. "Are you sure?"

"He's not on the committee and he came out carrying those two bags."

McCough looked at the bags on the pavement nearby. "You're sure those bags were in the offices?"

Rosetta took a deep breath. "Look in them, Felix." She tried to visualize "Tony Brown," to remember if he'd been wearing gloves. She wasn't sure, but thought he probably was. Nevertheless, "Take care about fingerprints."

McCough crouched by the closer bag. He took a pen from a pocket and used a pointy bit from the cover to hook the tab on the bag's zip. The zip was partly open anyway, and slid easily. He bent over. "I can't see."

"Do you have a torch?"

"Oh." He fiddled with a pocket.

"Give it to me. I'll hold it for you."

McCough handed her a small torch and he again looked in the bag. "Power tools," he said. "So you're saying these tools belonged to the Nation Day committee?"

"Look in the other bag."

The other bag contained money. Coins. Bags and bags of them. Perhaps too bulky or too heavy to take to a bank's night safe. "Oh my God," McCough said.

"Call for help, Felix. Get some people out here."

"Right." He reached for his radio.

"I'm going back to the committee room. It's unlocked. I want to make sure that nobody else goes in there."

"Good idea."

Rosetta quickly made her way back to the Nation Day HQ. She stepped inside and using only the back of a fingernail she flicked the light switch. She was not surprised when the lights in the room went on as usual.

But much in the room was not as usual. Drawers were open, chairs were pushed aside and there was rubble on a table.

And, in the ceiling there was a hole through which Rosetta could see the night sky. A square hole.

As Salvatore approached the family's house, a police car drove past him going the other way. But by the time he opened the door and climbed the stairs, he was lost in thought. A bit surprised, though, that no one was in the kitchen. He went to the living room. No one was there either. He dropped onto the couch for a moment, to think.

He wanted to tell someone about everything that had happened at the police station, *and* get an update on Marie. He'd expected at least one member of the family to be waiting up for his return.

Unless they weren't back yet. Was it bad news about Marie? Salvatore scrambled to find his phone. He dialled his brother's number.

After several rings Angelo answered. "Gina? What's happened?"

"No, no, it's me," Salvatore said. "How is she? Marie?"

After a moment Angelo said, "Fine. She's going to be fine. They're keeping her in till tomorrow."

Salvatore sank back on the couch. "That's a relief."

"Too right."

"Well, I've just come from Manvers Street. The cops are keeping Rafter overnight too. They found pills in his pockets. They're testing them."

"Good," Angelo said.

"They'll want to test Marie too."

"The hospital did that when we got there. Rohypnol doesn't show up in the blood for very long."

"You sound tired, bro."

"I was asleep."

"Where?"

"In my bed. Gina's staying with Marie. I came back."

"You're here?" Salvatore stood up. "Want a cup of tea?"

As Rosetta was being led to one interview room at Manvers Street, D.I. Phillips came out of another. "Bloody hell," he said. "*You* again?"

"There was a burglary at the offices of the Nation Day Committee," Felix McCough said.

"Confess now," the bulky D.I. said to Rosetta. "It'll go easier on you in the long run."

"No, no," McCough said. "Ms. Lunghi chased after the thief and not only got him to drop the money he stole, she managed to take a picture of him."

"*More* bloody pictures?" Phillips scowled.

"Since we've run into one another," Rosetta said, "may I confirm that Ms. Nolfi's solicitor was given prompt access to his client?"

Phillips's head twitched toward the room he'd just come out of. "He's in there now. But your brother's already satisfied himself that we obey the law here, Ms. Lunghi. Not just with Ms. Nolfi but with the other possible offender who we brought here from your house."

"The lowlife who gave my niece a date-rape drug."

"Allegedly. Although we did find a variety of pharmaceuticals in the pockets of the accused lowlife in question. They're at the lab."

"Another case?" McCough said.

"In every city, Felix," Phillips said, "there are a few families responsible for a disproportionate amount of the crime. I'm beginning to think these Lunghis are one of those families in Bath. Have we had *anything* through here today that hasn't involved them?"

"We don't *cause* the crimes," Rosetta said.

"Tell you what. To prove you're really the good guys, why don't you get the Nolfi woman to confess to killing her husband."

"Actually, there *is* something about that case I wanted to have a word with you about," Rosetta said.

"Oh yes?"

"It's just that when I was thinking through how Ms. Nolfi's ex-husband might have died, it occurred to me that it might be a good idea for you to check the stairwell in front of the building because—"

"First you give me work and then you tell me how to do my job? You're just taking the bloody piss now." Phillips stomped away.

10

Two evenings later Marie was home and feeling no lasting effects from her experiences with alcohol and Rohypnol. However, she was not a happy bunny. "I *thought*," she said to Jason, "that you arrived this much before dinnertime to see *me*."

"That too, of course," Jason said.

"That *too?*" Marie could not believe how cavalierly Jason was treating her. Here they were, alone together in a private place—her room—for the very first time *ever*. But instead of trying to hug her and kiss her or even just comfort her after what *could* have been the most traumatic incident of her *life*, all bloody Jason had on his mind was how he wanted to talk with her *grandfather*. "Either before dinner or after. Whatever suits him." It was *outrageous*.

Not that Marie would have let herself be hugged *or* kissed. Or that she really needed comforting. The episode with Rob Rafter was disturbing if she thought about it, but she didn't *remember* anything bad, so it was easy to ignore. But *Jason* shouldn't be ignoring it. He should be fluttering around her, seeking to mop her brow and satisfy her every whim. Instead, he was planning his networking encounter. Which made Marie *mad*.

At least it was good for one thing. If there'd been any lingering doubt that Jason was *not* the man for her, there wasn't now. How had she *ever* let herself fall for him in the first place, however prestigious a catch he was? The self-obsessed idiot never shut up!

"Marie?"

"*What?*"

"Why are you being like this?"

"Like what?"

"Getting the hump because I want to meet with your grand-father. You knew I want to get to know him. We talked about it."

"*We* didn't talk about any such thing," Marie said. "*You* talked about it. On and on and bloody on. Because all you talk about is yourself, Jason. *Your* plans, what *you* intend to do, what *you* want. You *never* show the slightest interest in *me.*"

"That's not true."

And now, *finally,* he stretched out his arms to hold her. Hah! Marie pulled back and brushed his hands away. "And let me save you some time. My grandfather will *not* want to waste any of his Tuesday evening with you."

"Well, we could arrange another day."

"He won't want to listen to you rabbit about your plans *any* time."

Jason stepped back as if he'd been slapped. "You can't know he wouldn't be interested in a young entrepreneur."

"Yes I can."

"You've told me yourself, he's a *businessman.*"

"He's *old,* for God's sake. Mum and Dad don't even let him do proper jobs in the agency anymore."

"But he has other commercial interests. The buildings he owns, shops he rents out in them, or whatever. And if he's not as active as he used to be then he might want someone to take an entrepreneurial role."

"A what?"

"That's like being an entrepreneur but from inside a company or corporation."

"What *corporation?* You're talking about my *grandfather,* Ja-son."

"Interacting with people who have new ideas must be second nature to him."

"It's second helpings that are second nature to him. You'd have better luck networking with David."

Jason hesitated. "David? Really? Because of his computer skills, you mean?"

"Honestly!"

There was a knock on Marie's door.

"Yeah?" she called.

"Dinner's soon," her mother said.

"Are all Cornish girls like you?" David sent.

"You're looking for more of us?" Lara answered. "Isn't one enough?"

"You are one-derful."

"Thanx."

"In all my years at that school I never even knew that staircase was there."

"You just never needed a quiet place to kiss somebody between classes before."

"Very true."

"Do you like kissing me?"

"Do you like kissing me?"

"I'll need more trials to confirm the promising early test results," Lara wrote.

"Thoroughness is *very* important in any research project."

"Oh oh, there's mum. Gotta go."

"X" David sent. He sighed. Then he sent, "XXXXXXX *hasta* later, perfesser."

He was wondering if she'd think he really didn't know how to spell "professor" when there was a knock on his door. What *now?* They were always knocking.

"David?"

His mother. *"What?"*

"Nearly dinner time."

"O-*K*," he called, although it came out more harshly than he'd intended. But if they *would* keep interrupting him . . .

Still, if Lara was away from the computer and doing something for her mum . . . David didn't yet understand why Lara's mother was so dependent on her daughter, although there were hints that her mother drank a lot. Her mother might even have been responsible for the bruise on Lara's cheek when they met before school on Monday. It hadn't been there on Friday and Lara would only say it wasn't important. Families were *so* complicated. Just look at the recent events in his own family.

Well, there would be time to learn about Lara's parents and other relatives. David no longer felt uncertainty about the little newcomer's feelings and the prospect of a long, delicious summer stretched before them.

Speaking of delicious, however . . . Lara's abrupt departures from the computer normally meant she was doing something that would take time. Perhaps making dinner? So, no harm his leaving his computer too, to eat with the family. As long as it didn't take too long. David got up and stepped out into the hall.

He'd expected to see his mother there. Instead, Jason brushed past. Behind him Marie was standing outside her room, hands on hips.

"Trouble in paradise?" David asked.

Gina knocked on Rosetta's door. From inside, her sister-in-law called, "Yeah?"

"Dinner's about ready, Rose." Gina put her head in. "Sorry it's a bit late."

"No problem." Rosetta sat on her bed and looked as if she

hadn't been awake long. "I should have been helping."

"After the three days you've had? I *don't* think so. And the only reason we're behind is that Mama wanted to make profiteroles for your friend, since he liked them so much on Sunday."

"Oops," Rosetta said.

"What?"

"I uninvited Laurence. I forgot to say."

"You *uninvited* him? Really?"

"A bit rude, I know, but Mama's purpose for having him here tonight wasn't really to show our appreciation for what he did for Marie, and I didn't want him to misinterpret anything."

Gina considered. "So you're not interested?"

"No."

"I thought maybe you were."

"Then I got to know him," Rosetta said. "That diminishes the allure of *so* many men."

Mama's profiteroles were done and waiting in the fridge. A double batch. She, however, was upstairs chivvying her husband. "Where are you?" she called. "Where are you that you're not downstairs banging your knife and fork on the table and waiting to be fed?"

"In a minute," the Old Man called from the bedroom.

But Mama didn't want a minute that might stretch to five, who knew? She went in and discovered her husband with the right sleeve of his shirt rolled up. He was making a muscle in the mirror.

"I'm still strong," he said.

"I know that."

"Even if they don't need me."

"Who doesn't need?" But she knew. That her husband did not have a more active part in the business he'd created continued to bother him. It bothered her too because it meant he stayed around and complained so much. "You *would* have gone to the prison. *They* didn't stop that. Circumstances caught up, that's all."

"Even Rose works on cases now."

"It just happened."

"Why doesn't it happen that *I* work on cases?"

"It happened that you tackled."

"So I should wait for it to happen some other time?" He rolled down his sleeve and buttoned the cuff. "How long can I wait at my age?"

"So don't wait."

He turned to her. "Retire? I would drive you crazy. Huh! Craz*ier.*"

"Did I say retire?"

"What then?"

"*Make* it happen. Open a branch. Advertise."

"Set up *new?*"

"I said a branch, not a tree. Advertise. Say, 'Specializing in detection for senior people.' They live longer these days. They have problems. And they don't like to ask help from condescending police and lawyers and teachers who all look like children. Let them talk to you instead. Let them hire investigations. You can find out which grandchild is worth the inheritance, or if the nurse just wants to marry for the house. Lots of old ones have the money to pay to a detective who is so strong."

The Old Man stared at her.

"What?" she asked.

"Not just a pretty face." He nodded. "I *could* become a branch, expand the business. Get rushed off my feet. Let them downstairs help only if *I* need."

"So *now* will you come to dinner, keep your strength up and share your wisdom with all these guests we have?"

"Wisdom? Was it *wise* of me to get so old?"

Mama felt a moment of tenderness. "Very wise."

Angelo was getting out plates to set the table with when Jason came into the kitchen from the bedroom corridor. He passed quickly through to the landing doorway. "Jason?" Angelo said.

"Oh, sorry Mr. Lunghi. But I've just had a text from my mother, and I'm afraid I can't stay for dinner after all."

"I hope nothing's seriously wrong."

"He's a self-centred pig," Marie said as she followed Jason into the kitchen. "That's pretty seriously wrong."

"Look in a mirror, Marie," Jason said. He vanished and headed down the stairs.

"What's *that* about?" Angelo asked his daughter.

"Nothing." Marie tossed her hair and held a hand up as if she were looking in a mirror. "Not bad. Not bad."

"I don't understand. I thought you and Jason were a couple."

"You're right, Pa."

"I am?"

"You don't understand."

11

"So where is our Salvatore?" Mama asked, her frustration growing. "Does *nobody* come to dinner tonight, after I expect so many?"

Rosetta and Gina exchanged looks. Marie said, "More food for the rest of us."

"More food is not the problem, young lady," Mama said. "Less people, that's the problem. Especially less Salvatore, after Rosetta decides she's so fussy about big." Mama sighed. "*And* you, Marie, with your Jason . . ."

Marie put the back of a hand to her forehead and sniffed delicately. "Oh, don't worry about *me*, Grandma."

"Drama queen," David said.

"Yes, I am rather a queen. I'm *so* glad you agree."

"I agree that you're selfish enough to *think* you're royalty."

"*David,*" Gina said. "Enough."

"Well she *is.*"

"No she's not, and in any case she needs a bit of consideration from the rest of us, after what she's been through."

"Getting drunk with strange men and being terminally stupid?"

"Honestly, David, I don't know what's got into you."

"Little *Lara's* got into him," Marie said. "And at least that's better than him getting into her."

"What is it tonight with you children?" Angelo said.

"Don't blame me, Pa. I can't help Davy's mood. He goes all

teenage when he's been up all night."

"Were you up again last night?" Angelo asked.

"Not *that* late," David said.

"All night every night," Marie said, "cyber-chatting away with his little cyber-friend. Pity she isn't real."

"She *is* real," David said. But then he regretted not having been able to come up with a counterattack rather than just a denial. He *was* tired.

"*If* she's real," Marie said, "why isn't she here tonight to share some of the wonderful food that Grandma and Mum have made for us all?"

"You have a friend?" Mama asked.

"It's a school night," David said. He was very close to bolting from the table to go and email Lara. At least from her there was nothing but support.

"There are buses," Marie said. "*As* she and the execrable Jason demonstrated on Sunday night. Now, if you're looking for someone who's selfish . . ."

Mama said, "You don't need this Jason now, Marie. You're young. You can wait."

"I'm waiting, all right. To be served some food."

"*Served?* It's *served* you want?"

"Only because I'm so hungry, Grandma. And because everything smells so totally wonderful. But I'll do it for myself if you'd prefer." Marie put her hand to her forehead again. She pushed her chair back an inch or two.

"I can fill a plate for my hungry granddaughter," Mama said, "but if I *serve*, do I at least get a tip?"

"Of course," Marie said. "Never go out of the house without lipstick."

"*Marie,*" Gina said. "Stop being cheeky."

David puffed his cheeks out at his sister.

"Maybe our Marie suffers from drug residues," the Old Man

said. "Maybe it affects the system to produce this cheek. Maybe you should come to the gym with me, Marie. Purge yourself."

"I'm sorry, Grandpa," Marie said sweetly. "I'm just feak and weeble from hunger and it affects my judgement."

"What judgement?" David said.

"What is this feak?" the Old Man asked.

Marie said, "Sorry, Gran. I don't mean to be rude."

"What is weeble?"

"So much you've been through, we can excuse," Mama said. "But what about Salvatore? Not here yet when already we're late starting? Gina? What *excuse* is there for him?"

"All I know is that he rang this afternoon and said he was coming, Mama. And he said that he'd be bringing someone."

"Sally's bringing someone?" Angelo said. "Who?"

"He didn't choose to confide that information," Gina said.

Mama glowed with the public repetition of what she now knew. It was the first time in months that her elder son would bring a guest. A *woman*, surely . . . had he *ever* brought a man? And after all his Heather-missing, this was a sign he was over Heather at last. So let him be late with this new woman. They could make an entrance. "We won't wait," she said.

With steaming food already on the table, waiting was not much of an option. But Mama's declaration got the plates and bowls moving. Soon everybody was served and beginning to eat.

"At least *I'm* here for dinner tonight, Mama," Rosetta said.

"Where else should you be on a Tuesday?" Mama said. Tuesday and Thursday nights were family meals, only to be missed for special reasons. Also Sunday afternoons. The loss for Walcot Nation Day still rankled. It was obvious from the tone in her voice.

"I thought for a while that I'd still be at Manvers Street," Rosetta said.

Angelo said, "Rose has spent so much time doing the police's work for them, I'm surprised they haven't recruited her."

"My *daughter*, a policeman? No, no," Mama said. "Although perhaps Rose will recruit for herself. What about that nice policeman who came here on Sunday, since you don't like the giant. What was his name?"

"I think you mean Officer McCough," Rosetta said. "And thank you for the suggestion, Mama, but no thank you."

"I despair," Mama said.

"Officer McCough needs a mother, not a woman. And mark my words, I am *finished* with mothering men."

Mama paused at the force of this statement, which she didn't recall her daughter making in such a way before. The other adults at the table also recognized it as something new, except the Old Man who said, "Who wants parmesan?"

"I do," Marie said.

"It's not only the police Rosetta does the job for," the Old Man said.

"Don't take *all* the parmesan, pigface," David said to his sister.

Rosetta frowned. "I don't understand what you mean, Papa."

"I *was* going to interview in prison, but now I don't. *And* Mama doesn't re-educate that Wigmore boy. Both because of you. That's what you said, wasn't it, Angelo?"

"I didn't mean that Rosetta would go *instead* of you, Papa," Angelo said.

"It's just that the case went in a different direction," Rosetta said. "So now neither of those visits is necessary." She turned to the table to declare something else new. "And, this afternoon the case was resolved. Anyone care to speculate?"

"This is the square-hole?" the Old Man said.

"Yes, Papa."

"The square hole has been filled?" David said.

Angelo said, "Are you saying that the police have identified the square-hole burglar?"

"This afternoon," Rosetta said.

"From your picture?"

"That put them on the track but they confirmed the ID in other ways."

"So the man you stopped outside the Nation Day office, this 'Tony Brown,' he is in custody now?" Gina asked.

"He is."

"Well done, Auntie Rose," Marie said.

"Thank you, Marie." Rosetta bowed her way around the table. "Thank you, one and all."

"And is he going to jail?" David asked.

"Now that is a question that I can't answer in a straight-forward manner."

"Interesting," Angelo said.

"And *is* the man in custody Mrs. Wigmore's son, Keith?" Gina asked.

"No, he is not." Rosetta smiled.

"So have we completed the job that Mrs. Wigmore hired us for?" Angelo asked. "Proving the square-hole crimes were not done by her son?"

"*We?*" Gina said.

"Rose is part of 'we'."

"Yes," Rosetta said. "*We* have proved the square-hole crimes were not done by Keith Wigmore. Nor were they connected to him in any way."

"So we can send an invoice?" the Old Man said. "This Mrs. Wigmore pays, yes?"

"We'll send an invoice, Papa," Angelo said.

Rosetta said, "But . . ."

"What is this 'but'?" the Old Man asked. "What's but about an invoice for work completed?"

"You're saying there's more?" Angelo asked.

"There's more."

"Is it something connected to David's asking whether your 'Tony Brown' is going to jail?"

"In part." Rosetta looked around the table. "But it might help you to know that there is now more than one man in custody."

"Even though 'Tony Brown' broke into the Nation offices alone, he worked with someone else?"

"Yes."

"He led the police to another man?" Gina said.

"One other man, so far."

"It's a team?" the Old Man said. "A team of square-holes? But that's so stupid."

"Only one man did the square-holes," Rosetta said. "In different ways he will probably lead the police to several other men but it's best if you only think about the first of the other men."

There was a moment of thinking but not much concluding. "What will help us?" Angelo said.

"Think about the crime," Rosetta said. "Square holes in roofs."

"On Sunday we thought about such a stupid MO," the Old Man said. "Holes that are stupid to cut if they already put the father in prison."

"Except the son *didn't* copy his father," Rosetta said. "So who do you think *would* be stupid enough to use the MO?"

There was a pause. "Well, we know that the guy who's already in jail uses it," David began, intending to add that his being in jail didn't necessarily make him a bad person. But David was interrupted.

"Exactly!" Rosetta said. "Nobody else *would* be stupid enough to use the MO. Nobody but Des Wigmore."

"But he's in jail," Angelo said.

Rosetta spread her hands. "The perfect alibi."

"*Alibi?*"

"A guard at the prison has been letting Des Wigmore out at night to commit burglaries. My 'Tony Brown' *is* Des Wigmore."

"How can this be, at a prison?" Mama asked.

"The police don't know the full story yet," Rosetta said. "There may be other guards involved too. But so far they've established that the guard who let Des out on Sunday night also did it with other prisoners before him. Unfortunately for the guard, this time he picked someone with a trademark MO."

"And that," Gina said, nodding, "is why 'Tony Brown' led the police to someone else—the guard—and maybe some others."

"Perhaps other guards, and perhaps the other prisoners who've since been released. And for what it's worth, Des Wigmore's story is that the guard threatened him with loss of remission if he didn't cooperate. It is pretty clear that the guard's been taking all or most of the profits."

"Well, well, well," Angelo said.

And at that moment there was a noise from downstairs.

Everyone at the table froze, listening. Because the dining room was farther from the stairway than the kitchen, it took more concentration to hear when someone was coming up the stairs. Someone, or some*two* . . .

"Is it really going to be all right?" Salvatore's guest asked as she began to climb.

"Of course."

"Are they expecting me?"

"Well, not you, specifically."

"Who, specifically?"

"They just know I'm bringing someone."

"After everything that's happened, I'd have thought I'd be

the last person they'd want to see."

"*I* want to see you," Salvatore said.

"That is quite different." She arrived at the top of the stairs. "Where now? And do we *have* to?"

"I'm surprised you're so nervous."

"The situation is not exactly a normal one."

"True."

"You know, Sal, suddenly I'm not all that hungry. Why don't I just wait here on the stairs until you're finished? I don't mind."

"If you're not hungry, then you'd better be ready to fake it. Mama watches how much food my guests eat."

"You've brought women to dine with your family before?"

"Once or twice."

"I'm shocked. And were these women who modelled for you, by any chance?"

"Some might have."

"Then don't plan on *my* posing for you."

"No problem, as long as you eat . . ."

"In the circumstances, I can't believe your mother or your family will approve of me. I think toleration is about all I can hope for."

Salvatore opened the door to the kitchen, but when his guest stepped past him, he took her by the waist. "I'm offering a bit more than toleration," he said.

As the family began to eat again, Gina reckoned she had a pretty good idea who Salvatore was bringing to the meal. And it was no surprise that they were late, given the history and the complications. They *might* even be out there deciding whether this was a good idea after all.

But Mama would be devastated if Salvatore bailed on the meal now. And, in any case, it's important to get past awkward transitions sooner rather than later, if life's to move forward. So

Gina stood.

"Where do you go?" Mama asked.

"To get more parmesan, and perhaps another bottle of wine."

Mama jumped up. "I'll come with you."

Gina put a hand on her mother-in-law's shoulder. Gently she said, "Let me do this, Mama. I will get them in here. Just be ready to be warm and welcoming. We have to look forward, not back."

Mama did not want to sit but then she thought about warm and welcoming, and forward not back. What else should she be to her son and his guest? Where else should she look?

Then the Old Man said, "Help me."

"How?"

"Pass the salt."

With Mama distracted, Gina left for the kitchen.

There the first thing she saw was Salvatore's back in the doorway. However, it didn't take long to see signs of life behind him. She heard billing and cooing. "Oh, for heaven's sake, Sally, can't it wait?"

Salvatore did not respond immediately to Gina's voice, but the woman did. She jumped away and into the kitchen. "Oh *God,*" she said. "What an awful way to meet someone."

Salvatore took the woman's hand. "This is my sister-in-law, Gina," he said.

But the guest was *not* who Gina was expecting. Her guess was that Salvatore was bringing Heather, the clues being that he'd announced on Sunday that she was in touch with him again then he was bringing a guest after months of not. Who else should she expect? It was a two plus two. Only this time there was no four.

"Who . . . who are *you?*" Gina asked.

Salvatore went around the table giving everybody's name. "And this," he said then, "this is Azaria."

"Hi." Azaria took the seat Salvatore held for her. "I've been lucky enough to meet Rosetta before, but it's a pleasure to meet the rest of you."

"You know our Rose?" Mama said as she scrutinized this new woman. Older than the usual, but beautiful—Salvatore always had an eye for beautiful. But could there still be children? It was hard to be sure. "Was this before you met my Salvatore?"

"Only by a few hours, Mrs. Lunghi. Rosetta was kind enough to arrange for a solicitor when I needed one and Sal showed up at the police station to check that everything was shipshape and Bristol fashion. Then yesterday he rang to see how things had gone. And one thing led to another." She spread her hands. "And here I am."

"A *solicitor?*" Mama looked at Rosetta.

Rosetta was more shocked than anyone to see who Salvatore's guest was. "Azaria is a client, Mama."

"A *client?*" Mama turned back to her son and his new woman.

"A client who owes her freedom to your lovely daughter, Mrs. Lunghi," Azaria said.

"Your *freedom?*"

The Old Man frowned. "How can Rose give freedom?"

"I was being held by the police because they suspected me of murder," Azaria said.

"*You* are the murder?" the Old Man said.

Angelo said, "Are we talking about the man who died in Cobham Court, Azaria?"

"The dead man was my ex-husband so naturally the police thought of me."

"But she's been completely exonerated," Salvatore said.

The Old Man said, "You didn't do the murder, so who did?"

"The police now believe that the man's death was an accident, Papa."

"Either an accident or negligence," Azaria said. "But definitely nothing to do with me."

"But how does Rose figure in your freedom?" Angelo asked.

"Yes," Rosetta said, "how *does* Rose figure in it? I spent a lot of yesterday and today at the police station, but not talking to them about Henry Daniels."

"Ah, but you *did* tell D.I. Phillips to look in the stairwell," Azaria said.

"And when they did they found a lot of interesting things," Salvatore said. "There was even an old microwave down there. Imagine the damage *that* could have done. Apparently some mad guy in the building does his tidying-up by heaving things out his window."

"But," Azaria said, "the important discovery was a piece of stone, a coping stone from the roof. It had blood on it. Henry's blood."

"Which stairwell are we talking about?" Rosetta said.

"The one for the building Henry died in front of. He must have been standing there, maybe looking up at my flat, when someone on the roof knocked the stone loose. It fell on his head and then down the stairs."

"The police are trying to find out who was on the roof during Nation Day," Salvatore said, "but they have no reason to believe anyone actually tried to kill Daniels. Access is from the top floor flat and that's let to students. They figure the students and their friends were partying. Maybe even too drunk to have realized that anything had happened."

"And nobody in Cobham Court notices this stone as it drops on a head?" Mama said. "How can *that* be?"

"The police will probably ask in the media for witnesses to come forward. But so much is going on during Nation Day they won't be surprised if nobody does. One theory is that the stone fell when there was a parade going by on Walcot Street. Wacky go-carts and belly-dancers were both scheduled for late in the afternoon and one of the officers thought some butterflies might have done an impromptu encore."

"Poor Henry," Azaria said.

"And well done, Rose," Gina said.

"Thank you," Rosetta said, although the stairwell she'd tried to encourage Phillips to examine was the one in front of Azaria's building, not the Nazi's. However, it did not seem quite the right moment to confess this.

"And so, Miss Azaria," Mama said, "welcome, now you're free and not a murderer. Are you hungry?"

"Famished," Azaria said.

"And let's get to know a bit more about you. Would I be right to think that you're a single woman now?"

ABOUT THE AUTHOR

Michael Z. Lewin has been a full-time writer since 1969. His first mystery, *Ask the Right Question,* was published in 1971 and was set in Indianapolis, where he grew up. It began the first modern private detective series to be set away from the coasts in middle America. Since that time he's written seven more novels in that series (including Five Star's *Eye Opener* in 2004) as well as many other mysteries set in Indianapolis and elsewhere. *Family Way* is the third novel in the Lunghi series, set in Bath, England, where Mike now lives. An Edgar nominee three times, he has won awards for his novels in Japan and Germany as well as the United States. He's written prize-winning short stories and also writes stage and radio drama, nonfiction, humor, puzzles, sonnets and shopping lists.